619 Sessions

Thoughts and Quotes *this* CEO Needed to Know

Alberta Johnson

ISBN: 978-0-578-53069-7

DEDICATION

For My Daughter

CONTENTS

ACKNOWLEDGMENTS

I would like to thank God.

1
PROLOGUE:

In a sea of girls named Alicia, Phylicia and Laticia (and the variant spellings), I used to hate my Old English name Alberta. Now when I tell people its meaning, I jokingly turn up my nose and say, "It means noble and brilliant." Session 07-04-2016 1:00 p.m. A child's name can have a direct effect on their destiny and I am going to live up to mine.

One goal, I want to see Alberta Johnson on a book cover. The quandary—how does one get there from here? 'Wasn't easy. I had to "find the place inside myself where nothing is impossible,"—Deepak Chopra. I love the arts—painting, music, literature, and dance. "Art is not what you see. Art is what you make other's see."—Edgar Degas. True art has heart! World Record holding Olympic Gold Medalist Michael Phelps believes, "Anything that you put your heart into—it's possible." That's the thing about art, this is my creativity and no one but I can create this. Anyone can write a book, but not *this* book!

It's wonderful to become inspired from the words of others. I only have blips of brilliance; but I can consume, digest and marry ideas. At first, I was journalizing what I reasoned miraculous. It blossomed from there. It's a documentation of my immaturity going towards being a little wiser though still naïve. It was difficult and I had to remind myself, "defeat is a state of mind; no one is ever defeated until defeat has been accepted as a reality."—Bruce Lee.

Ultimately, it's not about me; it is more about the quotes from others. Another goal is to share knowledge with everyone that will make a difference financially, physiologically and spiritually. My contemporaries will enjoy my flavor, my flow and the rhythm in many of my fluid sentences.

I'm confident most will enjoy the great quotes permeated. If you hold fast to your beliefs, I hope you will enjoy agreeing or disagreeing with what you choose. Yet remember, "A mind once stretch by a new idea never regains its original dimensions"—Oliver Wendell Holmes Jr. and "what we think determines what happens to us, so if we want to change our lives, we need to stretch our minds."—Wayne Dyer.

I aim to hold your attention from cover to cover. If not, why write? This is not about writing. This is not about book sells nor fame. This is about waking people up! My intention is to help people; otherwise, it would be as useless as a pointless pencil, sans eraser. This project will fill a niché. It is similar to John Bartlett's Collection of passages, phrases and proverbs, originally published in 1919, but my primary objective is to point to God. I too, as John Bartlett says, "have gathered a posy of other men's flowers and nothing but the thread that binds them is mine own." It's a lot of data that I have taken in, and reflected upon—many ideas inspired for God. It is my prayer that if there is more that is not of the will of God than there is for the will of God, may this text not be successful. I have made that statement because I am only human with human limitations and fallacies so please, "forgive me my nonsense as I also forgive the nonsense of those who think they talk sense,"—Robert Frost

A Reader's Digest clipping I have been saving reminds me "you have to be first, different, or great" and Loretta Lynn completes it saying, "If you're one of them, you may make it." This book is first and different serving as a book of quotes and memoir. As a motivational book, there has never been one serving a dual purpose.

I begin this story on what I've learned growing up during the rise of Hip Hop, 'poor—to upper poor' and semi-well educated. I hope these parts of me, coupled with the thoughts and ideas of others, can inspire you; give you reason to ponder. Before you read any further, I want to inform you that this will be the impetus to propel us out of the Spiritual Dark Ages!

Session 01-12-2008 6:19 a.m. I can assure you that they do not want you to know. They want to keep us confused with that ideology from the Dark Ages to facilitate keeping humankind in The Spiritual Dark Ages. They want us to believe science and/or knowledge and spirituality and/or religion are not related. They want to keep our focus from the true relationship we can have with The Creator and/or Creation enabling them to keep us in slavery (mental, financial or otherwise). To answer that timeless question, 'who are they?' I say—reflect on it.

I had intended to gather a great team of creative artist each having a genuine relationship with the one true living God. My Pastor said, "There are a number of possibilities when people come together." We are all inspired in our own individual ways from the living God who as The United Church of Christ proclaim, "Is still speaking." Unfortunately, no one had faith in me nor my ability to dream big then execute, so I must tackle it, as always, alone.

Tony Robbins is known to have said, "Never laugh at anyone's dreams. People who don't have dreams don't have much." Furthermore, Walt Disney reminds that, "all dreams come true . . . if we have the courage to pursue them." "All who have accomplished great things have had a great aim, have fixed their gaze on a goal which was high, one which sometimes seemed impossible," says Orison Marden Swett. "Whether you think you can or you think you can't, you are right."—Henry Ford. Connect those with having the faith to follow it through as the New King James Bible says in Isaiah 42 (paraphrased), "I have called you in righteousness and I will hold your hand to open blind eyes. My glory I will not give to another. The former things I declare; before they spring forth I tell you of them."

2
BERT I:
THE EARLY YEARS

I have a different understanding of God. For me to have come from point A to point B had to have come from an inner strength and desire of life to thrive—an inner strength placed there by The Creation. I developed different thought patterns because I had no one else. I, for the most part, was alone. I had to rely on the quotes of strangers because I gained nothing logical from anyone close to me. I remember times I have helped others because I thought it pleasing to God; then, I had no 'earthly' one to help me in any significant way without it being quid pro quo. From A to B without anyone had to have come from a higher power. I have a special relationship with Creation. I want to share it with you and for those who don't know—you can have it, too.

One may feel that no one is an island. Yet, I profess, as the girl that no one loved, that it is possible. Yesterday, September 20, 2008, I was attempting to recall a good memory. Randomly thinking about my childhood, I remember at age four being whipped for fidgeting by one of the teachers because I could not fall asleep at naptime. I remember being the little girl who wore an Afro to school one day in second grade and being sent back to school the next day without having my hair combed or braided. I do not remember being mocked; but it's evident because one of the third grade teachers combed my hair in front of her class. No one dared laugh in Mrs. Robinson's class. I remember my cousin coming to visit from her suburban life, and frequently punching me in the stomach. Eventually, I snapped and slapped her. After that she never punched me again! I remember being locked in the basement, in my eighth year. I even remember trying to get some candy that Barbara Ann had hid atop the cabinet after giving some to my brother and cousin. After I stepped down, I cut my left toes on a shortening can lid that had not been pushed into the container. After hearing me cry, Barbara Ann simply snatched the goodies from my hand and left me bleeding. Ironically, this may have been a life-extending event. Because of fear of can lids, I preferred liquid oils in bottles over hydrogenated.

I remember finding a one hundred dollar bill in an encyclopedia: I read them when bored. "The cure for boredom is curiosity. There is no cure for curiosity."—Dorothy Parker. Still having an innocent mind regarding thievery, I reported finding the money and had it taken away by the great-grand mother. I think I did get to go to Disney World. The trip overall was not memorable because the great-grand was miserly. My cousin and I were unsupervised at the pool and we dared each other to jump in on three. I jumped. She didn't. I recall seeing myself from outside myself face down just below the surface of the water. It was a woman who saved me. I remember one year, time sprang forward and I was left to fend for myself. I was sent to elementary school early for the free breakfast but the doors were locked. I ended up at a neighbor's in the 1200 block of Irving Street that sympathized with my situation and fed me breakfast. They were surprised I was left unattended. I did not remember that my friend, Danita, used to steal food and feed me. She remembered and reminded me one day as adults. I've kept in touch with her since kindergarten. I do remember the empty refrigerator and stealing food from it when there was some. Good ol' great-grand was always afraid we would run her to the poor house. I wonder what they were doing with the food stamps Barbara Ann received. I remember going to Sunday school and everyone was comparing the skin color on the outer arm with the inner forearm. My inner arm was filthy with dirt, only being allowed to take a bath on Saturday night. The great-grand had to put on a 'show' for church but didn't care if we were dirty during the week. My suburbanite cousin was with me that day—her arms were clean.

While Ma (grand-mother) was ducking and dodging fists, we were ducking and dodging extension cords. It was only once; but, my step-aunt even got a spanking with a water hose. I was thirteen while living with the stepfamily. They had weird ideas about personnel hygiene. I never saw the step granddad take a bath, only sink washes. He explained, "You can't get all the dirt out of your skin—God made you from dirt!" My ignorance was painful for those who had to smell me. I had poor hygiene too, though not as bad as the other family members did, or so I thought. That's debatable because one day we went swimming and a kid grabbed my ankle. Layers of old skin and dirt rolled down. After that embarrassment, I took one of the kitchen scrubbing sponges and kept it hidden for personal use. I've been exfoliating ever since. It wasn't long before they wondered why I didn't complain about being hot, as they did. One June, my step uncle was calling my step aunt dirty because she hadn't bathed since April. He took a bath in May—but it was June! I once leaned over her legs and thought, "Her knees even stink." On a positive note, I guess the water bill was low.

As I grew older, I became more tenacious. I coordinated a robbery of our home. My step aunt, step uncle and I pulled the ladder from under the house, placed it on the living room balcony and I climbed to the second floor and through the master bedroom window to steal eggs and white bread from a closet. Don't ask me why the eggs weren't refrigerated; but that was the best scrambled eggs on white bread and margarine sandwiches, ever.

As a dirty, scrawny, malnourished kid, of course, I was bullied. Bart walloped me in elementary. He punched me in the face and my head hit a cement wall. By the time I entered junior high school, I was savvy enough to find a way to get candy to share. That was my way of buying friends and staying off the radar. I had an incident with Tarica, which was my first fight. I can't say I won; but she didn't beat me up. She claimed she was slipping on the ice. Because her reputation was tarnished, she eventually challenged me to a rematch. It seemed like that second fight went on for half an hour, as no adults were around to intervene. It was a big show with a crowd of teenagers watching. Directly after, the 'cool' girls were looking for a reason to fight Reggina ("Everyone won't get that. That's for the scholars a hundred years from now"—Brian Griffin). They assumed she had been the instigator of the fight, so they attacked her. More likely, the girls were seeking a reason to jump her because she was cute and had the figure of a woman. It was probably a case of herd mentality as three girls attacked Reggina. She was being punched, kicked and stomped by three girls as she lay in a ball. As powerless as I was, I stopped that! It looked to be too much and my compassion for another human caused me to be brave enough to intervene. Surprisingly, it worked. It could have gone the other way. I could have been in a little ball on the ground next to her being pummeled. I look back and see that as a character moment. She got up and ran home crying to her older sister who was supposed to have been my best friend since kindergarten. Later that evening Danita came to my house to fight me. I can't say I won; I hid under the beds. I'd never forgive her for assuming I wanted her sister attacked instead of thanking me for helping her sister.

Two years later, my greatest fear was Joy; trust me—she was not. She was the bully that would put her hand in my pocket and take my money. I'd do nothing. If I were playing Ms. Pacman, she would push me aside and take over and I'd do nothing. She once coerced me to smoke the devil's lettuce with her and a couple of guys in Brentwood (now Brookland Manor), then tried to make me have sex with one of them. I thought, "I guess I'm going to the hospital today." That was a no go; but she didn't fight me. She was sexually unrestrained, while I still a virgin; though, I had probably already ruptured my hymen. A rumor that if one engages in intercourse one gains weight interested me. I had low self-esteem weighing ninety-nine pounds; so, while in junior high I would use a phallic shaped object in attempts of making myself 'fill out.' Dumb enough to believe that rumor; I reasoned my body would not know the difference between male parts and artificial ones. It didn't work. I remained a ninety-nine pound 'virgin'.

I once watched Joy fight Keila when there were only the three of us. Joy got Keila's arms pinned and was wailing on her face. I should have helped; but I was a coward. The final straw was at my home when I was straightening my hair with the hot comb. There were other witnesses; though, I don't remember why I had a group of girls watching me fry my hair. Joy said she would, "take that hot comb and put it on my face!" The little gremlin finally said, "Come outside." I had no choice. I wasn't going to let a bitch brand me. During the fight, I remembered how she pinned Keila, so I bucked as a bull and got her off me. I can't say I won; but she didn't beat me up. The neighborhood was buzzing with bewilderment, "Little Alberta gave the trollop a wallop?" It was no big deal and deep inside I still feared her.

I cannot recall any good memories and I do not recall having anyone close to me in life that has not hurt me. Having a mother (Barbara Ann) with a child's mind, an alcoholic grandmother, a miserly great-grand mother and a never heard of father, it seems I was doomed from the start. I guess that is why I assumed (most recently) that God loved me, because no one else did. I am the little crooked-faced girl that no one loved who must now "turn my wounds into wisdom."—Oprah Winfrey. "The way of the peaceful warrior is not easy, but happiness is not a simple quest and neither is love."—Manny KnightBlnc

Well, enough of the pity party, for now. Everyone has his or her own problems, and far more severe, in this day-to-day grind called life. "Life is a grindstone; whether it grinds you down or polishes you up depends on what you're made of"—Jacob M. Braude. "We are not held back by love we didn't receive in the past, but by the love we're not extending in the present"—Marianne Williamson.

3
1984

Sent to N.C. abruptly, away from everything that (though rough) was familiar. At the age of seventeen, I was slapped in the face with prejudice and racism never experienced growing up in predominately-black Washington, D.C. That's not 100 percent true. We had the typical lighter skinned versus darker skinned African-American issues but nothing like the prolific issues further south. I wrote the following poem following the cultural shock of N.C. The poem follows:

Why?
Why can't there be happiness spread throughout the land?
Why can't there be joy and peace for each and every man?
Why can't we live in peace, without any ridicule?
Why can't "Honor Love" be our golden rule?
Why can't we be free, from hardships, war and pain?
Why are happiness, peace and love such hard things to obtain?

The unhappiness reflected is a synopsis of things that have hurt me. I could not fathom the George Chakiris quote, "No matter how dark the moment, love and hope are always possible." "It is not easy to find happiness in ourselves, and it is not possible to find it elsewhere."—Agnes Repplier. The Dalai Lama advises, "If you want others to be happy, practice compassion; if you want to be happy, practice compassion." I had been sponsoring a child through Feed the Children for $18.00 per month. Unfortunately, that did not last long. I was earning a mere $3.35 per hour. Knowing the physical and moral weakness caused by hunger I attempted to help one less fortunate and it did give me some sense of purpose. Ann

Landers informs, "The true measure of a man is how he treats someone who can do him absolutely no good." "The more we give of anything, the more we shall get back," teaches Grace Speare.

Other than a few highlights, the eighties were a rough blur. I had a couple of white boys that wanted kisses in the basement of the fast food restaurant where we worked who would dare not be seen in public with. I guess it was curiosity about brown sugar. One other incident involved one of those Confederate flag flying guys, who was as cute as a button. He was not attracted to skin with heavy melanin. We, once, had an intense argument because he wasn't getting my customers' burger fast enough. After closing and clean up, I needed a ride home. He lived closest to my neighborhood and even he didn't think a young black girl should walk three miles home alone after 1:00 a.m. The ride was icy and quiet. I said, "Thanks." As I reached for the door handle of his car, he leaned over and placed a quick kiss on my cheek. I guess it was his way of apologizing (I knew I was right about that burger!). He may have wiped his lips on his sleeve as he drove away; but it was a beautiful human connection moment.

While working at the fast food restaurant, I met a guy from D.C. He and I went to the same high school, in the same year; but we never met at Coolidge. I thought it was fate that we met, so he was my first, as I thought, "we ain't going to be doing that all the time." Ignorance is painful, though my first time wasn't. It was about a year and a half relationship. I would open a can of ravioli and set up dinner by candlelight. Eventually, the cheating bastard gave me crabs. That almost drove me crazy because I was ignorant those matters, also. He lied about the source. Once he decided the ninety-nine pound former virgin wasn't good enough, he went on to bigger females that were more experienced. Funny, I read about the rhythm method but knew nothing of crabs. At the end of the relationship, I eventually got knocked up. I went to the emergency room and I learned of the pregnancy. What was scarier was the bill that was over a hundred dollars. I decided then, I can't afford it. I ran up the stairs and jumped down. I ran up the stairs and jumped down. I don't know if it was the cause; but, I had a miscarriage. It was a painful week in bed alone and for six months following that area reeked; but the body eventually healed itself.

Towards the end of 1986, I met the boy from New York City. He thought I was going to middle school though attending Barber-Scotia College. That should have been a sign. The day my right hand index finger gave the come-hither signal is the moment my life was horribly changed. This lying slick hustler was a pretty boy. He was the one who made tears roll down the sides of my face as opposed to the first boyfriend. His misadventures caught up with him and he was incarcerated from January 1987 until March 1988. I waited on my second lover to come home and immediately conceived. No one taught me Maya Angelou's insight, "When someone shows you who they are, believe them," so soon after, the cheating bastard gave me chlamydia, while I was carrying his child. What a fool—I waited! Had I access to a gun, people would have died! Fortunately, I didn't have the ability to make that decision.

Associating with the wrong crowd and being badly influenced, I broke the law. While in jail August 1988, a cellmate talked about free medical care at the health department. The first doctor's visit was the last week in September. She was born the second week of December. She was born into a notoriously bad family with terrible habits and horrible reputations. As a naïve new mother, I had a special pot used for sterilizing her bottles. I came home to find my daughters' family members taking over the house and cooking in my sterilizing pot. Angrily, I knocked it off the stove with the contents. This started a fight with the woman who eventually became my mother-in-law. I can't say I won; she did beat me up.

4
THE NINETIES

Between 1990 and 1999, I became somewhat stable working in the Mill, then the large tobacco factory in town. I completed two Associates degrees and began working on my Bachelor's degree. I probably wasn't the best mother working full time and going to college. Because of this, my daughter probably did not get the love she deserved. By 1999, life was improving, there were more times I gave thanks to God; though, not as much as I should have. I seldom prayed but when I did—I prayed for others. I lost faith in prayer when I asked God to give my friend a few more years with her husband. Lydia was at a low point in her life. At the same time, I was at a high point in mine, or so I thought. September 1999, I had the best first kiss of my life and I thought I had found earthly love, though it was only brief and fleeting. I was very happy, for the most part. I prayed what I thought was unselfishly saying, "Dear God, please let my friend's husband live—even if it means my love and I should separate." I guess I felt guilty for being happy while she was sad. Unfortunately, she lost her husband and I lost love. God did not accept the deal. Confused because things did not go my way, I became agnostic. People who have stronger faith would have likely seen it as God's plan for something better. It hurt my friend and it hurt me to see her hurting. At the time, she had a great job, excellent benefits, and she would be OK. I did see that she still had a blessed life. However, that was a major turning point. The faith in the power of prayer and in God answering prayers for me was significantly diminished.

"Where love is great, the littlest doubts are fear; when little fears grow great, little love grows there."—William Shakespeare. During the earthly love minute, I was at last happy; but since I had never been—I was afraid. I thought, "Surely I'm going to be in a fatal car crash." Does that make any sense? I am happy, yet full of fear because I had never known happiness. In addition, I had no one suitable to raise my daughter, if something were to happen. My ex-husband and his family had neither interest nor suitability to rear her. What a quandary. I have to live for my daughters' sake. Fear has no place in my life if I want to love freely. Fear is a spirit of evil. Shakespeare was right.

Once I lost my best first kisser, I only had work and going to school. I was finally fortunate and blessed with a good job, my own home, a healthy child, and the ability to help others; but even with those blessings, I was still not happy. In hindsight, I learned that faith, living my life knowing there was something better and a continuous relationship with God was missing. "The soul hardly every realizes it, but whether he is a believer or not, his loneliness is really a homesickness for God."—Hubert Van Zeller. Conversely, "The deepest sin against the human mind is to believe things without evidence."—Aldous Huxley

While attending my fourth college, I took the David A. Kolb's Learning-Style Inventory and my plot position on the graph was far from the center, which yields an inflexible learning style. My plotted position revealed I have a high percentile for Abstract Conceptualization (Thinking) and Reflective Observation (Watching). I fall into the Assimilator category, which means I am interested in the abstract and I like sound theories. My professor explained, "If the theory is not sound, I will throw it out," as he cast his arm exaggeratedly. According to Thomas Jefferson, "the moment a person forms a theory; his or her imagination sees in every object only the traits which favor that theory." Taking the Kolb inventory helped me to begin to understand myself. Once I began understanding myself, I had ready armor, offensive and defensive, when discussing God. If not for this new knowledge, I may have been unable to articulate, as well. I had to use my intellect even while Stip argued sternly that, "I can't understand God with my intellect."

While coming out of that confused state and before entering another, I eventually came to a place where I was in agreement with Charles Kimball. His quote, "I am convinced that it is possible to be a person of faith with integrity—a Christian, a Hindu, a Jew, a Muslim, a Buddhist—and at the same time recognize that one's own experience of God does not exhaust all the possibilities."

While I was gaining new knowledge in one area, I was still very much ignorant with how to be treated in relationships. The 1999 love I thought was real, because I was an adult and not a 17 or 21-year-old kid. My nonexistent experience and stunted growth with successful relationships (family, friends, and boys) caused me to lack the awareness that this, too, was leading nowhere. I could only create poetry for my first boyfriend after he caused me pain and the relationship was near an ending. I could only create a criminal record and a child with my second boyfriend/ex-husband. For my third love, I could only create poetry that conveyed my dependence on him for my own happiness. Therefore, after I found before losing him again, I had that creative passion and enjoyed writing little poems for Vaughn.

Happiness is a mystery
Far beyond what I can see
I've never known and do not now
I wish I did but don't know how
To gain that feeling of euphoria
I would, if I could see more of ya

Paul Cezanne said, "A work of Art which did not begin in emotion is not Art." I suppose I should thank God that I lost my earthly love. I could have never loved him properly, at that time. In retrospect, one should "never get too attached to anyone unless they also feel the same towards you because one-sided expectations can mentally destroy you."—Beautifulquotes.

5
BERT II:
FELT THE PRESENCE

After the mental destruction, I became more withdrawn. I learned, again, to rely on self and not trust others. "Just remaining quietly in the presence of God, listening to Him, being attentive to Him requires a lot of courage and know-how."—Thomas Merton. I had the courage; don't believe I had the know-how. The day that transformed my life happened in the Fall of 2003. I was pining away over my earthly love. Then, He came into my life and awakened me from darkness. "The deeper the grief, the closer is God!"—Fyodor Dostoevsky

The first conversation in thoughts occurred when crying out, "I love him so much it'll make an agnostic pray to God." God heard and answered. That is why I was moved when first hearing Casting Crowns sing a verse agreeing, "Still you hear me when I'm calling, Lord you catch me when I'm falling." God really did hear when calling and He caught me. I thank Him. Psalms 50:15 confirms, "And call upon me in the day of trouble, I will deliver you, and you will honor me."

The argument took place back and forth in thoughts one right after the other. I fought hard to reason that disagreeing was justified; but I lost the argument. It only took place in a matter of minutes; but in the end, I gave in and thought, "You're right." Following this enlightening exchange, I decided to take a shower. It was at this time that I received the most overwhelming feeling of joy. Acts 2:28, New King James, verifies my feeling because it reads, "You have made known to me the ways of life; You will make me full of joy in Your presence." With eyes closed, I saw the most beautiful bright warm white light. It was truly the best feeling on

Earth. The best I had ever experienced. I again tried to fight against it beginning to weep and hold my head down thinking, "but I love him so much." The joy poured over me again for another ten seconds to snap me into a happy reality. I have never been that morose again. Casting Crowns sing it best in a line from the song titled, '*Who am I?*' that goes, "Who am I that the voice that calmed the sea would call out through the rain and calm the storm in me." I told God in thought that it was so awesome, He need never to touch me like that again. I told Him if you ever feel the desire to bless me so generously, please give that feeling of Your presence to someone less fortunate. "That deep emotional conviction of the presence of a superior reasoning power, which is revealed in the incomprehensible universe, forms my idea of God."—Albert Einstein.

Overwhelmed by God's power, I could not keep silent on something so awesome. After sharing, Keyché said I was baptized in the water. Whatever the label I am truly blessed and thankful. I then shared the event with Jency and Sena. Call it coincidence; but they too have had similar encounters. It makes me smile to know that my friends know God. They confirm we should trust what we hear inaudibly.

TRUSTING WHAT WE HEAR, INAUDIBLY

"Converse with men makes sharp the glittering wit, But God to man doth speak in solitude."—John Stuart Blackie, *Highland Solitude*

One day at work, we were discussing astrological signs. I held no true value in the discussions: it's just entertainment. A supervisor commented, "Oh, you're a Gemini—you hear voices in your head don't you?" I looked perplexed and replied, "Oh, I thought that was God." The room got quiet. The evil spirit of doubt is a devil to me; though, I began doubting the insights that I had previously gained. On the ride home, I thought, maybe I am not being inspired from God; after all, I do not have a great family background. After work while at home "safe inside my room" crying that morning, I saw Christina's Aguilera's video, 'Trust the Voice Within' for the first time and when I needed it most. If you have a device near, take a listen.

When I heard her sing the words "don't cry" to a young girl, it caught my attention!

When I heard her singing about being in "your room," I really took notice.

She seemed to be singing directly to me when she had sung a "brighter day" is on the way.

Finally, she pointed directly at the camera and sang, "You know that I'm talking to you!"

The gist of the song, of course, is to trust whatever it is that we hear inaudibly.

"The more faithfully you listen to the voices within you, the better you will hear what is sounding outside"—Dag Hammarskjold. I knew, without a doubt, I was meant to hear Christina Aguilera's 'Trust the voice within' song on that day at that precise moment; but I could not explain that to the 'coincidence believers.' While reading Neal Donald Walschs' "Conversations with God—An Uncommon Dialogue," I discovered that there is someone else in the world who agrees and understands as I do. From his book, Neal Donald Walsch tells me that God told him, "This is not the only way I speak to you…Hear Me, everywhere …My response could be in an article already published, …In a movie now being made, …In the song just yesterday composed."[i] After reading page 210, I realized that his conversation with God revealed to him the same thing that was understood by me. I had an overwhelming realization that God was actively involved in my life that day to reassure me through a song that had already been written. Example below:

Whispers
The man whispered, "God, speak to me" and a
meadowlark sang
But, the man did not hear.
So the man yelled, "God, speak to me" and the thunder rolled across the sky.
But, the man did not listen.
The man looked around and said, "God, let me see you." And a star shined brightly.
But the man did not see…
So, the man cried out in despair, "Touch me God, and let me know You are here."
Whereupon, God reached down and touched the man. But, the man brushed the butterfly away, and walked on.

T. Lee Baumann, M.D. author of "The Akashic Light, Religion's Common Thread" has a quote from the Kabbalah, "Mind, Meditation, and Mystical Experience" Matt, Daniel C. *The Essential Kabbalah, op.cit,* pp. 124-5 that appropriately reads:

When you train yourself to hear the voice of God in everything, you attain the quintessence of the human spirit…[B]y training yourself to hear the voice of God in everything, the voice reveals itself to your mind as well.

[This citation is reminiscent of a passage from a popular Cayce text on meditation: "In prayer we speak to God; in meditation God speaks to us."]

"God whispers in your soul and speaks to your mind. Sometimes when you don't have time to listen, He has to throw a brick at you. It's your choice: Listen to the whisper, or wait for the brick."—Author Unknown.

God can do anything. Well, at least I believe it. God can use anything in His creation to get His point across—even our brains. Maybe I should not tell stories revealing madness and a sense of losing my grasp on reality. Then too, Jim Rohn said, "Imagination is the beginning of reality" and "Imagination is the reality of the dreamer."—Scott Ringenbach.

WHAT IS REALITY?

"Tomorrow changes the face of reality."—Philip Jose Farmer, *The Lovers*. "Our brains interpret the input from our sensory organs by making a model of the world. When such a model is successful at explaining events, we tend to attribute to it, and to the elements and concepts that constitute it, the quality of reality or absolute truth. But there may be different ways in which one could model the same physical situation, with each employing different fundamental elements and concepts. If two such physical theories or models accurately predict the same events, one cannot be said to be more real than the other; rather, we are free to use whichever model is most convenient."—Stephen Hawking & Leonard Mlodinow, *The Grand Design*

Session 06-19-2006

What is reality?
I make my own reality.
I create my reality,
By the choices my mind makes
By choosing what my mind believes
I create reality
For the eternal is one.

What is reality?
I make reality.
No, I create reality.
GOD creates reality
For the Eternal is One!
The Eternal is Everything.
Everything is One.
One.

Philip K. Dick says, "Reality is that which, when you stop believing in it doesn't go away." Though Gavin Freeman answers, "Reality is only for people with no imagination." Andre' Tarkovsky questions, "Where am I when I'm not in reality or in my imagination?"

The great Albert Einstein said, "Reality is merely an illusion, albeit a very persistent one" that is "subject to the mind's creation"—Diane Stein, *Essential Reiki.* "Every human being relies on and is bounded by his knowledge and experience to live. This is what we call 'reality'. However, knowledge and experience are ambiguous, thus reality can become illusion. Is it not possible to think that, all human beings are living in their assumptions?"—Itachi Uchiha, *Naruto: Shippūden*

"Reality is a formless lure,
And only when we know this
Do we dare to be unreal."—Maxwell Bodenheim, *"Dialogue Between a Past and Present Poet"*

Kenneth Boa author of *"Rewriting Your Broken Story,"* says of reality and hope, "You cannot live without some kind of hope, even if it's not founded in reality, because it is a necessity for life." "The people who say you are not facing reality actually mean that you are not facing their idea of reality. Reality is above all else a variable. With a firm enough commitment, you can sometimes create a reality, which did not exist before."—Margaret Halsey, *No Laughing Matter*

What is reality? I don't know; but, I do know that if I'm not happy with mine, I must change it. What is reality? It's happening as I create this sentence and as you in my foresight read it. After the quotes and my poem above, I must honestly answer that I still don't know.

WE DON'T KNOW WHAT WE DON'T KNOW

What I know wouldn't fill a thimble and neither would many in my circle. "If the true and ultimate reality is unknowable all reality is unknowable; what we take for reality is merely phenomenon, and what we take for knowledge is merely illusion."—Samuel Harris, *The Philosophical Basis of Theism*

We don't know what we may in the future learn in my lifetime or in many lifetimes. Five hundred to 1000 years from now, humankind may be looking back on us saying, "They didn't know that!" Just as we do when we look back on history and are critical. We also look back on many events in history with awe, as humankind may in the future do to us. Richard Dawkins said, in a Reader's Digest article Oct. 2013, "Science in the future is going to be revealing all sorts of things which we have no idea of at present . . . ." I argue if science in the future is going to do that, maybe one of those things will be a better understanding of God or the possibility of Intelligent Energy.

Session 07-17-2007 You think all there is—is all there is, when it's so much more. I found a note I had scribbled that also states, "We think we know…but we don't know what we don't know!"—Author Unknown. Another scribbled note states, "What we know is so much smaller than what we don't know."—Author Unknown. Further agreeing C. Simmons says, "A wise man knows his ignorance; a fool thinks he knows everything." "Good teachers are those who know how little they know. Bad teachers are those who think they know more than they don't know."—R. Verdi. Finally, some philosophy notes further expound below:

The most famous philosophical character of the classical world,

Socrates of Plato's dialogue, did not pride himself on how much he knew, but he prided himself on being the only one who knew how little he knew (reflection, again.) What he was good at (estimates of his success differ) was exposing the weaknesses of other peoples; claims to know. True knowledge exist in knowing you know nothing—Socrates.

"We are finite creatures trying to understand a highly complex world created by an infinite God (and)…many make the mistake of assuming that his or her individual perspective on an issue is comprehensive and exhaustive,"[ii] when we need to consider "there are also unknown unknowns."—U.S. Secretary of Defense, Donald Rumsfeld

It is important to keep an open mind about most matters, because recorded history tells us that man evolves mentally, physically and technologically. One other way just may be spiritually!

DELUSIONAL COINCIDENCES

"No man is happy without a delusion of some kind. Delusions are as necessary to our happiness as realities."—Christian Nevell Bovee. James Ellis puts this chapter in perspective saying, "We are always living under some delusion, and instead of taking things as they are, and making the best of them, we follow an ignis fatuus (something deluding, foolish fire), and lose, in its pursuit, the joy we might attain." To the believer's the signs *are* everywhere. To the doubter's we will call them delusions or coincidences.

A memorable event happened in February 2004 while watching a worship service. Exiting the bedroom heading towards the dining area, a cross of sunlight shined brightly on the wall. I was perplexed as I thought myself a Deist and not one who conforms to organized religion, though I indulged in various worship services sporadically.

Another coincidence occurred while watching a Joyce Meyer episode on VHS. I began daydreaming and became lost in thoughts about God's creation, and I was pleased with it all. While using my off the driven path logic the VHS tape stopped at the exact moment a televangelist on television was saying, "everybody won't see it the way you do."

A third coincidence occurred as I dreamt about Stip and me discussing God. In the dream, May 30, 2007, I said people would believe these interactions with God if I said, "If … Then … and the window slammed shut in the dream." At that moment, I was awakened by the noise of an overhead hair dryer hood falling. The responses that people gave after I explained the dream and how I was awakened varied. Lakena, a believer gets it. Stip for the most part gets it. Jency understood it or pretended to in order not to hurt my feelings, as did Shandra. Stefani got it significantly. She even said, "Yeah, He'll do it." Shandra remarked "He's tryin' to get your attention;" but, she doesn't know our relationship. He already has it.

There are so many doubters, especially Knox. This is surprising because we have had these types of discussions when I was first spiritually awakened. He said something about me 'getting signs' eventually after some skepticism. Yet, I do not refer to any of my interactions as mere 'signs,' because they are direct interaction in my life from the Creator of The Universe, the Holy Spirit, the Father or any of the 'labels' we give God.

One of the coincidences bordering on delusional occurred 07-29-2007 1:30 a.m. God used the moon to smile at me! He utilized the full moon and the clouds. When God uses physics (matter/energy, motion) in The Creation to smile while you are admiring God's handiwork, you have to tell someone. I told Jency, Lakena, Stip, Keyché and Havah. I received positive comments. Stip, initially, didn't believe me until he asked a couple of days later if, "I would want that to be one of the last moments that flashed through my mind," and I said an unhesitant, "Yes!" I spoke with a few of the other people and one comment (even after previously telling him about the overhead hair dryer falling) was a silly, "were you high." I thought what a silly question to ask when one is discussing the Maker of The Universe. I wish I had thought to tell him I only consume for entheogenic purposes and I do have a personal relationship with our Creator. Through the utilization of prayer, meditation and reflection at quiet times—I do get to a higher state of being. Yes, it is true. God utilized the full moon and the clouds that were passing by to smile at the precise moment I was thinking something I perceived would have made God smile, even if it was pareidolia. Session 8-25-2007 10:45 p.m. God can use anything in His creation to get his point across—even our brains.

I Can't Believe
I can't believe they can't look at the moon and see what I see

A piece of Creation—right before me
Something that was crafted with some of God's love
Something mystical, heavenly, and bright above
As a wide-eyed child, I gaze and stare
It's wonderful, marvelous and beyond compare

Session 10-08-2007 1:12 p.m. I was typing some notes in a chapter when I had ended the paragraph with the words Intelligent Designer! When I re-read it a cool autumn breeze burst through the windows and caused the flame on the candle to flicker harder. I thought, "You like that, don't you?" The leaves that had been stirred that were not in sight during the initial breezed drifted down as I looked through the windows. To some this may seem coincidental, but I see God's signs everywhere; in fact, I now look for them.

Session 10-21-2007 2:21 p.m. I told Lakena how I used my fingertip shadow to touch the shadow of a leaf reflection on the wall. As my finger tip shadow touched the leaf shadow, a breeze stirred outside and it moved. I snickered. Reflected and then I did it again. The branch and leaves moved again. I shared this story with Lakena and she decided she would try the same thing. Her event was similar. She touched a shadow of a tip of a branch and some birds flew out of the trees. Her next inner thought was, "You will soar."

Session 10-25-2007. I frequently step outside at work to discard the trash. It's an excuse to see what is going on in nature. I often think, "What ya got going on today?" I know it will always be something beautiful or a new surprise. I looked up at a beautiful sky line. A large bird seemed to appear out of nowhere. As I thought, dang that's a big 'ol bir- (I was in the middle of the word b-i-r-d) when I heard, "You will soar."

If you must conclude it is mere coincidence, it is better to believe the coincidences are direct interaction with God and have joy from the experience; because, "optimism can make you look stupid, but cynicism always makes you look cynical," says Calum Fisher. I once heard Bishop Eddie Long say, "You know how I know its God, because I can't explain it." I wholeheartedly agree with him because many of my personal experiences I can barely articulate. Someone once told me, "If you get peace from it you know its God." In the NKJ Bible Psalm 16:9 tells us, "Therefore my heart is glad, and my glory rejoices; my flesh also will rest in hope." I gain hope from my 'coincidences' for "hope is the anchor of the soul,"—Hebrews 6:19. Big Daddy Weave sings it best, "Every time I get another glimpse of your heart I realize it's true that You are so marvelous God."

When I re-read over my 'coincidences,' it overwhelms me, because I think, "You (God) did that for me." You showed these things to me to confirm that You are there. And you didn't have to do it—you simply did it because You love me. I can only lay my head down and think; I am so blessed. Those who do not believe have no idea what they are missing. It's His glory! It is truly True Love in the highest form (I think as I hear Toby Mack singing, "I was made to love you and be loved by You.") I cannot expect you to understand my view of any of the glory that God has shown me because, "nothing is real to you until you experience it, otherwise, it's just hearsay."—Author Unknown. Albert Einstein reminds, "Coincidence is God's way of remaining anonymous."

"There are No real coincidences in life for those with faith strong enough to recognize coincidences for what they really are: intricate pieces of the providential design God created for each of our lives" — Delia Parr, Love's First Bloom. "Coincidences mean you're on the right path."—Simon Van Booy, Love Begins in Winter: Five Stories. "Some people hear their own inner voices with great clearness. And they live by what they hear. Such people become crazy . . . or they become legend."—Jim Harrison.

NEVER ALONE

Session 12-06-2007. The One God in the manifestation of the Holy Spirit descended above me. I saw it in the cat's eyes. I was leaning over the left arm of the love seat playing with Pickles. In a matter of moments, I noticed him looking intensely above me to my left and waving his tail rhythmically. Because I feel good with my spiritual journey, I had no fear. I just took in the moment. I then slowly turned my head upward and to my left. There was nothing. I looked back down at Pickles and he had turned his head towards my right. I decided to let to moment stand, and did not look over my right side because I would not have seen anything. It was in the cat's eyes!

MY JOY

My ideas about Jesus began to change with age and reflection. I have matured in my spiritual relationship with God through the teachings of Jesus Christ. It was later, when I realized that I had to reason out why I believe the way I do and it had to make sense—not simply trusting familial tradition. I reasoned that if I say God can do anything then I must accept the fact that:

God can turn Himself into Jesus and walk amongst us.

God can use the Holy Spirit to impregnate a virgin and have an only begotten Son.

God can inspire and awaken Jesus as God has done many other prophets.

God can do anything.

God can.

God can…

If I am to say God, Creator of The Universe everything known and unknown, can do anything; any one of those scenarios is possible. Jesus is my Savior, because I was raised under his teachings. It is his teachings that have saved me and pointed to God in the correct way and cause me to want to be more as they say he carried himself. Without reasoning, it confused me to simply trust in authority figures. Especially since, I had never had reason to trust many authority figures. Furthermore, because of my learning style and everything that makes me—me, I had to utilize reason and I have now found the path to peace. Robert Frost said, "There may be little or much beyond the grave, but the strong are saying nothing until they see." Paul says in one of his epistles, "Prove not some things but all things and hold fast to that which is true."—1 Thessalonians. "Listen to all, plucking a feather from every passing goose, but follow no one absolutely" is a Chinese proverb that agrees with George Iles, who said, "Doubt is the beginning, not the end of wisdom." "Unanswered questions are far less dangerous than unquestioned answers"—Author Unknown.

I learned that personal beliefs have a direct influence on how one reasons. Stanly Grenz comments, "regardless of religious orientation, a person's basic beliefs (worldview) affect his or her way of life."[iii] I learned, also, to further understand personal beliefs and their influence on how a person reasons, I must understand presuppositions. "Presuppositions are those beliefs that a person generally holds unreflectively,"[iv] reveals, Darwin Glassford. While learning this ideology, I was taught how the relevance of beliefs to personal life is tremendous and how ones' beliefs shape how one reasons—positive or negative. In Created for Community, Grenz agrees imparting, "And these beliefs form the foundation for how we live." He further says, "Although all persons have beliefs, many people give little thought to how they form their fundamental convictions. And they rarely reflect on how these convictions are affecting the way they live." Proverbs twenty-three suggests, "As a man thinks in his heart, so he is."

Session 02-20-2007 5:45 p.m. God said to me, I understand you, you have to learn to understand yourself. I hear the Inner Voice, as many others. In Ephesians 6:19, Paul asked, "for prayer that utterance, words, sounds, expressions or remarks be given to him." Mary McLoud Bethune has a similar insight that concurs, "Herein dwells the still small voice to which my spiritual self is attuned."

THE RIGHT TEACHINGS CHANGE LIFE

My life began to change when I heard Joyce Meyer state, "It's not about me." Matthew 6:21 advises us, "Where your treasure is there your heart will be also." My treasure is now in trying to be pleasing to God and to ask God to use me in ways that I could have never imagined, as Joyce Meyer asked. In Paul's first letter to John in the second chapter, he tells tell us, "If anyone loves the world (material things), the love of the Father is not in him…and (worldly) desires pass away, but the man who does the will of God lives forever." If your treasure is in money, materialism, greed, selfishness just to name a few—your heart is there, too. How can God utilize a heart as this to promote a Godly mission? The same mission Jesus told us about over 2000 years ago. I believe God would want us guide the course towards a better future, before the next 2000 years. I am beginning to understand and I want to stay on the right path for The Creator.

"Imagination engages the deepest part of our being, and it is there the spiritual self resides," affirms Patrice Vecchione. Religious dogma has so many confused that it inhibits their inner creativity. The innermost part of being that is essentially a piece of God. The religious industry is confusing and the disagreements between many of our world religions and even the differences in Christian faith both Catholic and Protestant are confusing us when they all should be unanimously pointing to God. This industry has partitioned each other into little boxes and if you are not in 'this box', you are wrong. One cannot put God into a box. He won't stay or more accurately, It won't fit.

"Where there is unity there is always victory."—Publilius Syrus. Paul's letter to the Ephesians chapter four gives instructions on how to 'point' to God. It states, "It was He who gave some to be apostles, some to be prophets, some to be evangelists, and some to be pastors and teachers, to prepare God's people for works of service…until we all reach *unity* (author's italics) in the faith and in the knowledge…and become mature, attaining to the whole measure of the fullness of Christ" as his life represents how we should work for God. The job of those five aforementioned offices is to empower people to help others.

Session 06-19-2007. The First Corinthians 6:19 gives the lesson, "Do you not know that your bodies are temples of the Holy Spirit, who is in you, whom you have received from God? You are not your own." "It does not matter, for He has power over everything—the forces of nature and even our brains."—Author Unknown "Man's steps are ordered by the Lord. How then can a man understand his way?"[v] John 15:5 agreeing says, "Apart from Me you can do nothing." Jesus proclaims, "…that they all may be one, as You Father *are* in Me, and I in You; that they also may be one in Us, …" in John 17. Luke 17 also proclaims in verse 21, "The kingdom of God is within you." "The moment I have realized God sitting in the temple of every human body, the moment I stand in reverence before every human being and see God in him – that moment I am free from bondage, everything that binds vanishes, and I am free."—Swami Vivekananda.

DEVIL OR SPIRITS OF EVIL

In my circle of associates, many argue on matters concerning 'the devil.' For me, there is no devil; but I realized fear is a spirit of evil. I was scared to tell it. Scared to share insights for fear of people thinking I'm foolish. Things that distract us from God are spirits of evil—spirit as in the Zeitgeist meaning not apparition. Some examples are fear, materialism, greed, lust, and vanity just to name a few.

Common sense tells me that the Almighty, All Present, All Loving Creator of everything known and unknown would not create a direct opposite of himself. Why is there a belief that God, the only Creator, would create a 'being' as powerful as God? It does not make sense. I'm saddened for those who believe our beautiful world God created is, as Stip nonsensically spews, "The devil's realm!" I agree as Joyce Meyer taught, "He wants to have relationships with us."

I decided to look up a few scriptures on 'the devil' because my friend Stip told me that this is, "the god with a little 'g's' realm" and another friend of mine brought me a copied page referring to the many scriptures associated with Satan. I was thinking, "Can you bring me something that points to the goodness of God instead?" It's funny; I have actually had people get mad at me for not believing in their 'devil.'

> I cannot conceive of a God who rewards and punishes his creatures, or has a will of the type of which we are conscious in ourselves. An individual who should survive his physical death is also beyond my comprehension, nor do I wish it otherwise; such notions are for the fears or absurd egoism of feeble souls.—Albert Einstein

666

Session 06-06-2006 6:19 a.m. A few in my circle of associates caused me to reflect on the number. I had to make what I considered their view—logical to me. "You will die but the carbon will not; its career does not end with you. It will return to the soil, and there a plant may take it up again in time, sending it once more on a cycle of plant and animal life."—Jacob Bronowski.

> "Almost all the molecules a cell makes are composed of carbon atoms bonded to one another and to atoms of other elements. Carbon is unparalleled in its ability to form large, diverse molecules. Next to water, compounds containing carbon are the most common substance in living organisms. Compounds synthesized by cells and containing carbon are known as organic compounds. Well over two million organic compounds are known, and chemists identify more each day." [vi]

After watching the movie "Blood Diamond," I have decided I shall not wear a mined diamond. Not after the misery and suffering that is upon other humans over tightly compressed carbon. I *may* wear a man-made diamond. After leaving this earthly vessel and returning, in spirit, to the Oneness that is The Universe I desire for the cremains to become a fabricated diamond. Alan Bradley had this similar line of thinking saying, "Diamonds were nothing more than carbon, but carbon in a crystal lattice that made it the hardest known mineral in nature. That was the way we all were headed. I was sure of it. We were destined to be diamonds!"

With the new technology, it is possible. In fact, wouldn't it be ironic if that will be the future way of burial. The cost should diminish. I imagine a few thousand years from now they may be laughing at us. So many people spend so much money on a carbon based mineral when we have fellow men homeless and hungry. When the future brings wealth, I do not wish to be caught up in that materialism when I can use the financial blessings to help feed the hungry as directed in Matthew Twenty-five. I shall not fear the number 666, nor words.

WORDS ENLIGHTEN

KRS-One raps, "You know, you don't see with your eyes, you see with your brain and the more words your brain has the more things you can see." Words are a gift to us from God, through which we communicate with Him and each other. John 1 of the Bible tells us, "In the beginning there was the Word, the Word was with God, and the Word was God." Surprisingly, physics has agreed with biblical ideology, in a sense.

> Having seen particles first become symbols and then become bit patterns in a Continuum Quantum Computer, having seen the interactions between bit patterns similarly reduced to bit patterns we now come to the conclusion that The Universe and its physical laws—Reality—is in essence linguistic—Language.—Stephen Blaha, *The Metatheory of Physics Theories*

Most everyone knows words have power and Suze Orman elaborates, "Words become actions; actions become habits; and habits become destiny." The puzzle fits together, clearly. Create your destiny. Plan it then execute. It all begins with the thoughts converted into words. The words you receive are best discerned at quiet times. "Silence is the entrance into the deepest experience of being . . ."—Robert Sardello. Ralph Waldo Emerson tells us, "Let us be silent that we may hear the whisper of God." The great Mahatma Gandhi agrees in one of his quotes saying, "In the attitude of silence the soul finds the path in a clearer light, and what is elusive and deceptive resolves itself into crystal clearness."

I found Aaron Shust might have the same opinion, "But the noise of our lives and our misguided attempts to find validation elsewhere often deafen us from hearing His words of affirmation." The artist Immortal Technique advises us when he raps, "turn off the news, and read, read, read." After reading—reflect, in silence. Utilizing your mind, the thoughts and words you conceive can create your destiny. "Whatever the mind can conceive and believe it can achieve,"—Napoleon Hill; but also remember, "Motivation is what gets you started. Habit is what keeps you going," says Jim Ryun.

Session 05-07-2007 The New King James version of the Bible in James states, "…receive with meekness the <u>implanted</u> word, which is able to save your souls."[vii] The NIV Bible says virtually the same, "…humbly accept the word planted in you, which can save you."[viii] The Amplified text concurs, "…receive and welcome the Word which implanted and rooted [in your hearts] contains the power to save your souls."[ix] Now here's the kicker! If one, "in the beginning was the Word, and the Word was with God, and the Word *was* God,"[x] two the Word was and/or is already implanted, planted, grafted into me and/or my heart and three Jesus taught, "I am in you and You are in me, Father may they be one in us,"[xi] it stands to reason that it is truth. God is there, if we believe The Word.

I have always admired the giants from past centuries. The creativity springing from the Elizabethan and/or Renaissance periods from Copernicus, Galileo, Shakespeare, Bach, and Newton just to name a few is amazing. I am thankful God gave us the ability to receive knowledge through the ages from words. The inspired artist and talented scientist had a thought in their mind and centuries later, in most cases through words or the language of music, transferred to me are their thoughts.

THE MATHEMATICAL POSSIBILITIES OF TOO MANY THOUGHTS

Psalm 19:14 reads, "May my spoken words and unspoken thoughts be pleasing even to You, O Lord my Rock and my Redeemer." TLB I know traditional Christianity and the general message in '*The Secret*' is mostly opposing; but I like to put puzzles together. On October 2, 2007, I heard Joel Osteen say on Enjoying Everyday Life, "We draw to us what we think about…when you worry you draw in a lot of worries." That is nearly verbatim to some of the concepts in *The Secret.* I have a Heartland Sampler Moments calendar page that quotes, "Your brain is no stronger than its weakest "think."

Check this out! It is in '*The Secret*' and defined by other sources that the average human processes 10,000 thoughts per day. Ten thousand thoughts per day, multiplied by 365 days per year, multiplied by an average life of 82 years—that's a lot of thoughts. Now, check this! The bible tells us that God knows our every thought before we even know them and God knows our heart. Phil Joel agrees in his song titled, 'God is watching over you' with the song-lyric, "knows what you're thinking all the time." Finally, there are over 6 billion of us on *this* planet revolving around our star. Additionally, there are 50 to 100 Billion (known) galaxies containing one Septillion (10^{24}) stars speculatively with planets and possibly inhabitants capable of more thoughts *per* day and God knows *our* every thought before we even think them! As Chris Tomlin sings, "You put the stars in the sky and You know them by name." Then just how many thoughts per day does God have?

Session 09-24-2007. One day a couple of weeks later, I was pondering. How does God keep up with so much data? My next thought, "It's easy." Quit trying to make having a relationship with the Creator of everything known and unknown complicated; God knows we are stupid, comparatively speaking. Utilize the K.I.S.S. principle. We cannot fathom The God intelligence. *Everything* we think we know, God knows and for God it is *easy.*

Another way to look at it is if the average human processes 10,000 thoughts per day and you look at the world and the many things that are troubling, it gives reason for one to wonder how many of the 10,000 thoughts are negative. Stip told me, "If you are in a discussion and the first thing that comes out of one of the participants mouths is something negative then that tells him that that person is having a heck of a lot of negativity within their thoughts." Stip further commented, "When something negative is always the *first* response it is no wonder the world is in such dire circumstance." "Life has indeed, many ills, but the mind that views every object in its most cheering aspect, and every doubtful dispensation as replete with latent good, bears within itself a powerful and perpetual antidote."—Lydia H Sigourney

The process for changing some of those negative thoughts is easy. James A Baldwin has, "always believed that you can think positive just as well as you can think negative." If you evaluate then eliminate all the negative 'stuff' you are putting in, you will reap better output in dreams and also regarding what your first response may be. "How precious also are Your thoughts to me, O God."—Psalm 139:17 "You are never alone when accompanied by pleasant thoughts."—Author Unknown from Moments Sampler

Session 10-27-2008 5:40 pm. It has been a very interesting couple of days. I was relaxing and reading "Conversations with God" by Neale Donald Walsh and I gained some revelations when I utilized his information coupled with information I gained watching a video on mathematics titled "Life by the Numbers –A New Age—Information Age" with Danny Glover. In Neale's book, he mentions that God only created the two emotional forces Love and Fear. "Everything we do is either motivated by one of those two emotions," says Neale says God. Concurring appropriately Oprah Winfrey has said, "I believe that every single event in life happens as an opportunity to choose love over fear."

From "Life by the Numbers," I learned some information on the complexity yet simplicity of mathematics. The video delved into the topic of data mining and how it is graphed saying, "When you look at the data the right way then some patterns begin to emerge." One Mathematician and Economist, Graciela Chichilnisky of Columbia University tells viewers this information "can be used to understand the forces shaping the future to see where we're going, what's happening and why." She begins by creating a three dimensional graph and she says, "By studying the cones she believes she can see some of the profound changes that await us in the next age."

The social media platforms have the ability and are most likely utilizing our data in such a way. If they can analyze the motives of everything motivated by Love or fear from gathering information then over time they can see patterns emerging, as Graciela Chichilnisky teaches. If we change ourselves by being more altruistic the data will lean more towards love; thus, overpowering the data motivated by fear. We could change the world if we collectively change our words. Moreover, it's measurable via social media data mining.

We must change the data inputs so that which adds up to Love overpowers that which adds up to fear. If we can focus our energy into that which is motivated by love, we can change the state of the world. An electrical impulse in the brain is the same energy that created this sentence. Turn that energy into good thoughts and actions, and we can overpower fear and begin the awakening that will propel us out of The Spiritual Dark Ages! "What lies in our power to do, lies in our power not to do"—Aristotle.

SPENDING TIME WITH THE TINIEST OF CREATURES

I watched Albert Gore's "Inconvenient Truth" and learned of our probable fate so I decided to walk to the post office rather than drive. Alone on walks I enjoy time with God. I had passed a series anthills. Assessing the location in the cracked foundation of an abandoned building, I thought, "How are they finding food?" I had taken several steps while searching my pockets for a candy bar. I decided to back track, break off small pieces, and disperse them upon each hill. I walked and smiled thinking, "It's like manna from heaven." I felt kind sharing a snack with ants. That is life, too. I hoped this small act is pleasing to God. I could be wrong; but "What you have done for the least of these, you have done for Me," applies. As I walked, my imagination ran wild; but it's not a bad thing because "Imagination is the beginning of creation. You imagine what you desire, you will what you imagine, and at last you create what you will," says George Bernard Shaw.

I played this entertaining conversation out in my head as I headed towards the library. One lone scout ant happens to check to see why the ceiling is falling in. He discovers the tasty delight and runs to tell the others. He says, 'hey guys it's a big pile of food right outside the exit.' The others ragged him saying get outta here man. He says, 'No, seriously there is a big pile of food out there and we need to get started breaking it down before it gets dark and cold—for night will soon be approaching.' After enough coaxing the others follow, discover the manna and begin breaking it down. Later that night, they discuss it and one says to another, 'Do you think there is something bigger than us out there?' Coincidentally, that Wednesday, during Spiritual Cinema Circle the Spiritual Leader mentioned something about, "Spending time with the tiniest of creatures."

On the journey, I ran into my friend, Jency. We stopped and chatted a bit. Our conversations had been limited because she was waiting on a new cell phone. We parted ways and I continued on to the library to skim the newest Astronomy and Anthropological magazines. I read a sentence in the May issue of Astronomy, "The Universe is self-contained but we don't know what that means." I thought that's God!

Leaving the library the walk back home was rewarding. I revisited the anthills to see if they had made the discovery. They did and I was pleased. I was happy and believing that today, God is pleased with my spirit.

Session 04-16-2007 8:50 p.m. I was thinking, "If I was well-off I could feed the ants, donate money to charity, walk on the beach and relate to God. Then my inner voice whispered, "I need you to have relationships with others." I realized, "Yeah, that's true. How would I do that if I stay to myself?" I heard internally, "You need to talk to Jency, like you did the other day with Stip because she needs you, too." When these thoughts had adjourned, I noticed that four pictures had slid out of the book titled, "The Hidden Face of God." Taken in February 2004, the pictures were of the sunlight image that looked like a cross on the kitchen wall. Others call these events coincidences; but I really believed it was a 'sign' from The Creation. On this day, I had turned off the computer and I was not waiting for emails from anyone. I had the television turned off, as well. Lesson learned. Minimize distractions. I said it yesterday while helping my daughter with a school project, "it makes me wonder if our creativity is stifled due to so much outside interferences, which leaves us little time for reflection."

Session 04-16-2007 9:20 p.m. My thoughts, "You are an inspired one, you all are!" I smoked a bit of a cig and thought cancer, not me—you need me. No! I have asked to be used. "Now, you've got it!" God's beauty is infinite. God's love is infinite. God's power is infinite. God is the infinite One, the eternal one—One.

MY FIRST DING

Session 04-20-2007 3:00 a.m. I was praising God and thinking I'd really like to hear the Clark Sisters' song "You bought the sunshine" on my way to work in the morning. I then thought, some of that music I'm not feeling. At the time, I was under the covers in a dark room with no lights, no TV and eyes closed as I saw a speck of light flash in my left eye and I heard in thought, "sometimes it's for others." This was my first 'ding' but at the time, I did not have a word for it. In our discussion Wednesday, while viewing Juanita Bynums DVD, Jency said, "that in a message some things are for others." I am certain that needed to be reinforced, thus my first 'ding' coupled with a thought. At the time, I did not understand the 'eye flash' speck of light.

Session 04-21-2007 While giving Lakena an update on the ideas that have been flowing through my mind, I had discussed the little speck of light intending for her to understand that it was confirmation. Surprisingly she said, "Yeah, that's your ding." I said, "Huh?" She said, "I told you about it." Vaguely recalling the conversation, she continued, "A 'ding' is when she knows she is dead on point about an issue." Before discovering the 'ding,' I had believed God would use signs that were more concrete such as seeing photos that slid out of a book coinciding with a spiritual thought; an actual cross of light from the sunshine centered on the wall or catching a video at the most appropriate time.

Does everyone have a ding? Don't know, yet. One of Paul's letters documents that all have been given spiritual gifts from the Holy Spirit. "There are different kinds of gifts, but the same Spirit . . . There are different kinds of working, but the same God works all of them in all men . . . To one wisdom, to one knowledge, to another faith . . . all these are the work of one and the same Spirit, and he gives them to each one, just as he determines."

What can be made of this speck of bright light Lakena and I call a ding? A common sense analogy is to look at what occurs in our lives today. Humans have created the Internet and cell phone technology and new technology is getting more sophisticated every day. If I can send an idea from my head to an instant messaging program via wire or wireless to a tower, etc., and have it, interpreted by the human receiver, if we can do that can God not do so much more? If we can transmit a thought from one brain to another through centuries—can God not transmit a thought to our brain? Why, then, is it difficult to believe God relates to those of us who love God because The Creator first loved us?

DISCUSSING GOD AND SPIRITUAL GIFTS

Session 04-21-2007 5:47 a.m. The first note is from Havah. She said, "You know how we just discussed how God works in our lives. I told you that your focus should be on God and how you live for Him. The example we were discussing was how God will provide a partner in your life. You do not have to seek him out. You shouldn't spend your time thinking of what you want and you definitely shouldn't worry because you don't have what you want. This conversation started because some feel I should ask for what I want and God will bless me." Havah continued, "My opinion is firm. I was already blessed with my husband for believing the way that I do. God knows my heart and when I live for Him he will bless me. I would be selfish to ask anything from Him when I don't always put Him first. Thank you for being in my life at the right time. God has worked through you and my family to bring my focus back towards Him and my blessing is that after so many years of trying on my time, God has given me a blessing His. If this is not a lesson on patience and trust, I don't know what is?"

My reply was, "That's wonderful. God is doing miraculous things this week! Guess who I visited over the weekend? Vaughn and I realize that I still love him. While visiting I thought, or God inspired me to take some notes. We will talk Monday.

Session 04-21-2007 06:17 a.m. In an email to Jency regarding spiritual gifts I typed, I found it fascinating that you have the insights about color. That is your spiritual gift as we all have our own unique gifts from God. Isn't it ironic that you are so happy working around colors and shades? Maybe not ironic but destined. Denis Waitley said you should, "learn from the past, set vivid detailed goals for the future, and live in the only moment of time over which you have any control: now." I remember several years ago, talking about how I plan for the future. You said, "2008? I don't look that far ahead." I have went so far to plan that if I don't get two million, my contingent plan is to have over $400,000 in my profit sharing plan, $2,000 per month pension, my house paid for, retire at 55 and work another job after retirement from our company to earn more money to donate to charity, church and helping God's mission. I planned that a long time ago, when I learned of the pension plan payouts. I've been planning for a while. "If you fail to plan, you plan to fail."—W. Clement Stone. Conversely, at the Artbeat reminds, "As much as you want to plan your life, it has a way of surprising you with unexpected things that will make you happier than you originally planned. That's what you call God's will."

Session 04-22-2007. Over the weekend, I visited my earthly love and had a wonderful time communicating. While there, I prayed for God to use me in a way that I can't even dare to imagine, an insight from Joyce Meyer. I am a morning person; so, while he was sleeping, trains of thoughts raced through my mind. The first being, "I've got to do something (about our poverty)," as I gazed lovingly into his beautiful sleeping face. Love or lack thereof is a powerful motivator.

Suddenly, I realized all of the talented people I know that know God. Furthermore, we have all been discussing God with each other. Havah had said, "where there are two or more gathered in My name you're havin' church." Matthew 18:20 says, "For where two or three are gathered together in My name, I am there in the midst of them."

The second speck of light flash in my eye occurred and the concept for this text was developed. The idea was so BIG that my hands were trembling as I took notes and telephoned my best friend, Jency, to tell her the good news. While on the phone, I got a third speck of light as I described the project. It was the brightest white light, like a tiny star in a flash. She began to be on board; but current situations were keeping her from total focus on the idea. She was supposed to have been sharing her insights in sessions throughout this book; but it never materialized.

Later that morning, I left my love. While riding home I thought, "This will be the impetus to propel us out of the Spiritual Dark Ages." I have been working on this project ever since. I began Saturday morning, April 21, 2007, worked off and on through the night, took a break to go to church and I'm still at it. Without being preoccupied trying to relive moments with Vaughn, I can work for God.

I attended a local church on Sunday, April 22, 2007 and I had a wonderful learning experience. In Sunday school, the pastor asked the group did anything stick out in your head this week. I told the Pastor my sentence. I said, "This will be the impetus to propel us out of the spiritual dark ages." He replied, "Wow, that's profound." I love it when I get an Atta boy from my spiritual leader. He is a wonderful teacher. Our prayer of Confession went as follows: "… Help us to know that it is only in giving up our SENSE of control over our lives and following wherever you lead that we gain our lives. In the name of the One who calls us to pray. Amen." I see how this fits into what I typed last night. Believing that statement of faith, we say we give up our sense of control over our lives, thus we gain our lives coincides with the fact that He Reigns. I looked up every synonym for the word reigns and most point to the fact that reigning is to be in charge; time in power, period of influence, supremacy, sovereignty, be in power and most importantly, for this discussion—control. You are not your own because the Lord is in control i.e. "He reigns."

If I am not my own, who am I? Casting Crowns answers very well in their song lyrics. Here is a portion quoted below:

Who am I that the Lord of all the earth would care to know my name
Would care to feel my hurt
. . .
I am a flower quickly fading here today and gone tomorrow
a wave tossed in the ocean
A vapor in the wind

Agreeably, Mercy Me sings, "God With Us." If you have a device nearby, have a listen. I'll wait.

". . .
Like hinges straining from the weight, my heart no longer can keep from singing:
All that is within me cries for you alone be glorified Emmanuel. God with us."—Mercy Me

"Immanuel (Hebrew עִמָּנוּאֵל meaning, "God with us;" also Romanized as Emmanuel or Imanu'el) is a Hebrew name which appears in The Old Testament book of Isaiah chapters seven and eight. This was the foretold name of the Messiah.

Session 04-23-2007 4:32 p.m. I have lost, Havah, a person I initially thought might be interested in this project. I shared with her what I learned from my Pastor. He taught us that the prayer Jesus taught, "Our Father who art in heaven . . ." is meant to be used when you cannot come up with the words on your own. I shared this information with her based on one of our previous conversations. There in the midst of telling her, I saw my 'ding' and I told her. Unfortunately, she did not get it. More likely, she thought I was being irrational. She was neither interested in participation nor moved by any of my insights. At least, she motivated me and God has blessed her with joy. I assume she is scared: scared to look beyond her narrow religious focus to the spiritual—the metaphysical. She must continue with her concept that God is (what I think she believes) a 'man' and not a powerful force. My pastor once told us, "God will not be confined by our limited understanding." I thought she was irrational when she once told me, "God changed." I thought, "Huh?" She elaborated, "Yes, when you look at the Old Testament versus the New Testament . . ." I replied, "No, man's perception of God changed." Henry David Thoreau sees eye to eye, "Things do not change; we change."

Session 05-25-2007 4:06 a.m. I finally thought, "You were created for something greater and you can't achieve it if you don't put emphasis on the right source." My cousin emailed a 'Daily Motivator' that further emphasizes. Read how to "Focus on it" below:

> The influence of anything in your life is determined primarily by the amount of focus you give to it. Your focus can make things bigger or smaller, depending on its direction and intensity…and you can choose at any time to put that power to use. By directing your focus, you can positively affect every corner of your life. Focus on the world you would most like to see, and with the power of focus you will make it appear.

PREPARING ME MENTALLY

Session 06-24-2007 8:55 p.m. I was listening to a song by Tobi Mack titled, '*Made to Love.*' He sings, "I will give up everything for You, I'd give it all away." I realized what a bold statement that is to profess to give up everything for God. I decided to 'keep it real' and I thought in prayer, "Shoot, I wouldn't want to be homeless 'cause a sista' likes to take a bath or shower every day." I continued to imagine all that I would give up for God. I thought my house (as long as I had a small place where I can eat, bathe and sleep), my car and car payments, my current job (I reasoned I could work at McDonalds and not be homeless.) I agreed with the singer and I could give it all away, just as long as I am not homeless. Louis Pasteur understood over a century ago that, "chance favors the prepared mind."

Session 06-26-2007 7:15 a.m. Twenty-five hundred lives and our plans have changed. Our CEO had a big announcement that totally shut down production operations at the factory. We heard it for the first time. Our factory is closing and consolidating operations in another state. Well, I said I was willing to give up some things and I was well prepared by the grace of God, beforehand. On that day, I wanted to say something to ease the minds of my co-workers; but, I had to ask a question to gain the microphone. After my non-important question was answered, I told our CEO and the audience, "When God closes one door He opens another. I've enjoyed the ride."

It was a slow and calculated factory shut down. At work, the morale was gloomy and indecisive. Some were deciding to follow the company and move. Some were deciding to leave the company; but we were all going to be uprooted.

Session 07-21-2007 11:46 p.m. Conversing with Havah, she again stated, "How silly I was." I answered, "Yes, it does seem impossible to believe that I can write a book." I would not let her opinion sway me as I remind myself to "slay the naysayer." Havah did have one cool insight that I will add on her behalf. She said, "Every one of the 2,500 people affected by the lay-off is supposed to get something from this from God."

THE 'BAND-AID' FIX

Session 07-29-2007. If that dead squirrel in the road had to feel pain, who am I that I shan't? We all have our journeys on the road of life, no matter how unusual, which will include heartache. We all have our own pains—except, if we don't experience God the pain is more difficult to bear and we'll learn nothing. Had I not been going through such pain, I may not have experienced such a spiritual awakening. It took some time but I finally realized that even if I never share a life with Vaughn the pain was all worth it to gain God. On the other side of trials lies growth. Once I realized I'm supposed to put God first I included The Creator when I wrote to Vaughn.

There are many conversations I have wanted to have with you

So often, I wanted to say my love is sincere and true

But long nights of thoughts coupled with bad advice

I didn't know what to do

I thought, "If I had told you at an inappropriate time"

You'd turn and run away then never, ever be mine

Then everything that I would say and some things I would do

Would contradict how true and deeply I felt for you

Many years have passed and I have grown and become mature

I no longer have fear and doubt, I believe my heart is pure

GOD is the one who will show

The things I need to know

When I was hurting for you tremendously

It was GOD who called to me

He widened my narrow focus, and now I more clearly see

That I can, too, Love you; but, FIRST Love GOD and me!

It would have been a quick fix; but would not have dealt with core problem if my earthly love had had the kindness to show me a little love. In my confused state, I needed the strength and love of something more powerful than a mere man. I NEEDED GOD. It took a while but I know God awakened me when I was at my lowest point. I thought, "I awakened you when you needed to be awakened." Therefore, I know I was in a bad place. I thank God for the lost love and the pain that followed because it brought about tremendous growth—spiritual and otherwise. "All things work together for the glory of God to those who love Him…," indicates Romans 8:28

Session 08-12-2007 1:00 a.m. Emotionally, ignorance is painful. I realized why this man had to be continuously removed from my life. First, "If a man wants you, nothing can keep him away: if he doesn't want you, nothing can make him stay."—Oprah Winfrey. Second, I totally focused on him. Losing him did help my spiritual growth after my breaking point and the joy that poured over me in 2003. Before that, I believed in God because as a child I thought I heard His voice say, "I am your Father." After that, I remember telling Jency that it's all capital letters; bold and underlined BELIEVE in God. I had to learn to put God first all the time (which I'm still working on) and not fixate on my earthly love. God took the back seat anytime I visited Vaughn because, though short-lived it was very powerful, (the magnetism) when I was next to him.

Robert Frost made known, "Love is an irresistible desire to be irresistible desired." "Then the lover, who is true and no counterfeit, must of necessity be loved by his love."—Plato. Dostoevsky proclaimed, "To love someone means to see him as God intended him." "Beloved, let us love one another, for love is from God and everyone who loves is born of God and knows God." 1John 4:7 NASB

I looked to an earthly love for happiness but had to learn that true happiness comes from God. There is a far greater love and happiness in having love for the Great One. I was behaving as G.W. Von Leibnitz is quoted saying, "To love is to place our happiness in the happiness of another." Unfortunately, I was having disastrous results. "Most folks are about as happy as they make up their minds to be," expressed Abraham Lincoln.

"Where there is love there is life."—Mahatma Gandhi

"The greatest pleasure of life is love."—William Temple

"Once you have learned to love, you will have learned to live."—Unknown

Session 08-12-2007—Ten words for God

I never knew

Love so true

'til I found You

I realized that I love God; yet, I do not always love me. Once the love of God and the love of myself meet, it will make for a heck of a day.

I APOLOGIZED

Session 09-06-2007 5:45 p.m. Today is the day I finally apologized to God. As my eyes bugged out, and my eyebrows rose nearly to my hairline, I realized all that time I was fixated upon my earthly love; obsessing over bad decisions, and consumed with bitterness—I was supposed to be focusing on building and having an intimate and personal relationship with our Lord and Creator. I had to say I'm sorry. I'm sorry I wasted *our* time. Most recently, I have been able to profess, "I love You" wholeheartedly but I did not realize that I owed God an apology. "I was so stupid," I thought and my inner voice says, "No, you were in Spiritual Darkness:" I now know all that energy could have been utilized for God. "You live and learn, learn then know then know and grow."—Author Unknown.

Session 09-06-2007 5:59 p.m. My next train of thoughts was how much more before we're done and I realized, it doesn't matter, I am the creator and an inner voice echoed, "I am The Creator." Wow! God is in me and I am in God.

THE OXYGEN MECHANISM

Session 09-14-2007 11:10 p.m. The oxygen mechanism lets us know that God loves us so much that He gave us a perpetual oxygen mechanism. The Intelligent Designer of The Universe, creator of everything known and unknown, created the trees and plants I see that are making the oxygen used by me. God gave us life sustaining nourishment and oxygen from artwork. It is perpetual that we inhale O_2 and exhale CO_2 for the plants and trees that they may live. What a cycle. What a Creator. What a Genius!

What is the significance of the matter? In the end what does it matter? "Unless you assume a God the question of life's purpose is meaningless," says Bertrand Russell. Whether it is the 'Big Bang,' Creationism, Intelligent Design, what else could make matter think? Colin McGinn *The Unbridgeable Gulf* in Time has an answer. He says, "The answer lies in ourselves: our brains have not evolved the equipment to resolve this mystery. They go blank when they try to understand how they produce the awareness that is our prized essence." Page seventeen of that same issue also teaches that 78% of the brain is water, fats make up 12%, proteins 8% and the rest is salt and carbohydrates." This is the recipe used to make matter reason. However, the manifestation of the Spirit makes the inanimate animate. I reason it's for a reason.

Session 09-29-2007 5:31a.m. An America on line user answered another user in such a way that it captured my attention. After seeing his answer, I would not feel so alone in thinking so differently from acquaintances. Here are our comments below:

Hmrmdy 8:27:57 PM Sep 28 2007
it does not contradict it at all. I guess I left out the fact priori...
this "force" was intelligent.
but it was alone.
it de-evolved into atoms and molecules, using it's presence of mind to create fields of energy, magnetic fields, and allowed itself to become what we see as inanimate objects, rocks, plants, water, etc.
thru this de-evolution, God lent his life, his love to everything in this universe...
but in so doing, he still could not speak...
he could not see.
Then he finally created the first being with eyes..
and he saw his creation...

then he dreamed up more and more complex beings until he could actually become a mobile, seeing, hearing, experiencing, and communicating being. Man.
Now, as man stops being so selfish, and realizes they are all simply pieces of God, then together, we will achieve a cosmic awareness, and remember who we are...
I believe in God, but not some old dude sitting on a throne with His staff.... LOL
And I believe Jesus Christ was a *realized* Son of God, who died and went to Hell (the creation of evil minds trying to dissolve their sins)
He taught us that thru "WAKING UP" we could be one with God.
As each of us realizes our own faults, our own potential, and the fact that every other man is simply another version of ourselves trying to find the truth, we will join in one mind someday.
And God will be solidified into the entire Universe as one mind....
and what eternal peace we will feel...
....................after that?
I guess we get bored, and do it all again..
OR..
maybe there's another God out there, who we can fall in love with?
and we can make baby Universes...
and watch them become self-aware...

IamThe1Johnson [8:33 P.M.]: great reply to jcsgs11.
Anytime you wish to share those types of insights, please feel free to email or IM.
Thanks for Thinking. Smile
Hmrmdy [8:36 P.M.]: yeah, I should start a website..
Hmrmdy [8:36 P.M.]: but sometimes I feel I am so full of it..LOL
IamThe1Johnson [8:36 P.M.]: You really should
IamThe1Johnson [8:36 P.M.]: No, you are awake
Hmrmdy [8:36 P.M.]: trying...
Hmrmdy [8:36 P.M.]: not quite there...
Hmrmdy [8:36 P.M.]: thanks for the positive input..
Hmrmdy [8:37 P.M.]: stay awake as well. :)
IamThe1Johnson [8:37 P.M.]: I will. Never want it any other way now that I am.

The energy is the same at the atomic level that creates stars and us. That could sum up both scriptures created in His own image and I am in you and You are in me! Couple that statement with energy never dies it is only transferred or transformed. If it never dies, it is eternal meaning everlasting Life!

The Essentials Physics I, published by Research & Education Association, on page thirty-three, tells us, "The total energy—kinetic plus potential plus internal plus all other forms of energy—must remain constant, i.e., energy may be transformed from one kind to another, but it cannot be created or destroyed." Matter and energy have become alive and aware and we are the manifestation of energy cognizant. Dr. Francis Collins clarifies, "Energy and matter cannot create itself; therefore, it must be a creator our God" the original artist.

6
PRAISING THE ORIGINAL ARTIST

Session 10-08-2007. Confucius say, "Everything has beauty but not everyone can see;" though, how can one look at the horizon before the sun breaks and not see the beautiful art He gave us? All other art is merely a copy of everything He did. We can do nothing original without some form of imitating His art. He gave us free art exhibits daily. Every day for the rest of your life, you can marvel at the beauty in creation. "An early morning walk is a blessing for the whole day,"—Henry David Thoreau

This morning God asked me to take a walk with Him. I didn't interact with Him. I simply observed His handiwork. Take a stroll on a cool autumn morning before the Sun breaks the horizon. Today, 6:50ish a.m., I see Orion; Betelgeuse; Orion's belt pointing to Sirius; and other than Betelgeuse, apparently some other Red Giant (I don't think it is Mars). I am strolling south. To the left I see the waning moon. It looks like a smile today and above that smile to the right is Venus. Just to the left and above the pair was Saturn, I learned that in retrospect when checking an Astronomy calendar. I thought it was a star.

The cool breeze and the sounds of nature (crickets and birds chirping) make beautiful music. The striking green trees and flowering plants have reason. All this art is free from God. It is art with a purpose. God made artwork functional. It gives us food and oxygen. What a genius! What an Intelligent Designer!

Then, I hear the ugly noise. I hear someone's Central Air kick on. It's cool this morning, brainiac, open the windows and get the free air. I hear a noisy car driving. Our noise—the noise that we have created is nauseating. I just walked past freshly laid blacktop—the smell is nauseating.

We have to have homes. We have managed to change the environment to suit us. We have learned to make things better, quicker, and dirtier for the world to conform to us. I guess some is necessary for our survival as a species; but it looks like our brains are getting us into trouble. Hearing the noise and smelling the stench makes me wonder if early-man had it better. Shoot, it is October 8th, (What we used to call autumn in 2007. It used to be the time of year between the heat of summer as it faded into the cold of winter) yesterday and the day before it was freaking hot! I don't know the current hourly time—I'm still strolling.

I cannot see Orion anymore nor his belt. I still see Sirius, the other Red Giant (or is that Mars?) and the Crescent moon smiling with Venus to the right above it winking. It's almost like a 'ding.' The Sun is rising—no, we are spinning around towards our star.

"No thanks," I say and "keep riding weirdo," I think. Some dude just circled the block to offer a ride. I had no fear because I'm under divine protection. The Holy Qur'an 46:13 says, (author's italics) "Verily, those who say 'Allah is our Lord,' *(God is God)* then remain steadfast (in their belief) shall have nothing to fear nor shall they grieve."

A little later, a memory resurfaced of a childhood song, "He walks with me and He talks with me and He tells me I am His own." You remember it. It's daylight. I can barely find Venus and the Crescent moon because it's now bright. Here comes the sun. It's going to be a good one. The gentleman that offered a ride earlier just beeped as he rode back north—guess he *was* being sincere. I smile; yet cringe—I smell fresh blacktop again.

OUR PURPOSE

Session 10-24-2007. We are supposed to be helping each other towards a common goal. When people whimper, "Why does God allow…? Why does God let…?" They think the 'bad' has something to do with God. All the while we are supposed to be helping each other towards a common goal—a peaceful, healthy existence while here and developing an intimate and personal relationship with our Creator. When one is hungry, dirty and cold or unloved by society, the basic needs are not met. The basics must be met first in order to attain higher levels of Maslow's hierarchy. If it were possible to get worldwide basic needs met we can all achieve a higher level of self-awareness; thus, opening the doors for a true intimate and personal relationship with The Creator. When we help each other, we are helping other parts of our collective whole. This is the common goal. "To work for the common good is the greatest religion," says Albert Schweitzer. Richard Dawkins believes, "It is true that the moral standards of a society progress with great speed," so it is doable if everyone minimizes greed and excess. Furthermore, in GOD according to God, Schroeder states, "God created this world with a wisdom that realizes the pleasure of the body can take the spirit of the soul to heights the soul can never reach on its own." How could this possibly be achieved when the lower levels of the hierarchy are not met?

I know God is, from personal experiences. I know The Presence is shown to me through scientific knowledge and utilizing intellect. I know of God's existence through the many signs, the inner voice, and by using common sense. I have *faith* in knowing I am correct in my assessment.

MY PURPOSE

"The only person you are destined to become is the person you decide to be."—Ralph Waldo Emerson. Every trial, every obstacle, every heartache, every book, every class and even a part time job have all culminated with me figuring out my purpose. While putting together some of the pieces of my life, I realized:
The way I excelled at reading relative to the rest of my classmates
The times I spent reading encyclopedias in the basement of my D.C. home
The many books I kept long overdue from the local public library
The many fictitious names I created to obtain more books from the public library
The confusion and having no one to help me iron out the kinks
The part of me that is D.C.
The part of me formed in N.C.
The history of the sciences and how they have fascinated me
The history of those who went against traditional thinking that awe me
The part-time Co-op job where I assisted in editing
The Women's Studies class at UNC-Charlotte
The Philosophy class at Montreat College
The many scribbled notes of quotes that reminded me to keep my head up
The sadness that broke me and prompted my spiritual awakening
The fact that, though confused, I never denied the existence of a Creator

That list above has directed me to the place I am today. I know what my purpose is. This is! I'm going to play the hand I'm dealt. I will follow advice from Hannibal that goes, "We will either find a way or make one." I'll, too, remember, "Great things are not done by impulse, but by a series of small things brought together,"—Vincent Van Gogh

"Whether you think you can or you think you can't, you are right."—Henry Ford. A true testament to validate any claims I make will be made known to the world once this ideology and associated missions come to fruition. John shows me in Revelations 2:23, "All the churches will know that I Am The One who searches minds and hearts, and I will give to each of you as your works deserve." Time will tell, if I am doing God's will. Jesus also told his disciples, "And now I have told you before it comes, that when it does come to pass, you may believe."

QUESTION

Session 01-02-2008 9:22 a.m. In business, it is taught to ask the five whys to get to a root cause. For those who hold their beliefs unreflectively, they should ask them because anything important is worth questioning. One needs to get to the point where one is a thinker and not a follower. That is true reflection and newly realized knowledge. Eliminate brain washing. Seek reflection then realization. "I do not feel obliged to believe that the same God who has endowed us with senses, reason and intellect has intended us to forgo their use."—Galileo Galilei. One doesn't find God by 'what everybody else says.' One finds God by oneself. You find God by yourself. I found someone who agrees with me. Phineas Fletcher, The Purple Island agreeing affirms, "The way to God is by ourselves."

The following are examples of how I have answered the five ways:

1. Why do you believe the way you do?

Because I've examined my belief system.

2. Why?

Because I have an inquisitive mind and I chose not to believe everything placed before me.

3. Why?

Because, I had no reason to trust authority figures.

4. Why?

Because humans have fallacies.

5. Why?

Because only God is all-knowing.

--

1. Why do you think you're right about your beliefs?

Because I trust my experience of The Creation more than someone else's experience and I believe my personal assessment of my relationship with The Creation is correct.

2. Why?

Because I don't trust all authority figures and other humans have fallacies, which could be more erroneous than my own.

3. Why?

Because I surmise my own belief system has fewer fallacies than that of others.

4. Why?

Because no one else's assessment matters—whether I'm right or wrong.

5. Why?

A quote circulating on social media says it best, "Worry about your own sins. You will not be asked about mine."—Author Unknown

SOAR

Session 02-06-2008. In life, we will use some effort, get some rest and soar effortlessly. I was looking to the sky and admiring the view when I saw a few small birds flapping away on the mild winter day. I thought, I'm kind of use to seeing the birds soar, now. As I watched the smaller birds exerting more effort, I saw a robin perched atop a pole resting. Finally, three larger birds soared into view. My new insight is that in life we will use some effort, get some rest and soar effortlessly. I thought the soaring effortlessly would mean I had finally arrived. Apparently, it means I will still be doing work. It will simply be easier. The robin represents the rest. I was confusing soaring effortlessly with rest. Soaring effortlessly will still be work. "The man who has no imagination has no wings."—Muhammad Ali

Session 03-28-2008. I believe in my ability to soar. I have faith that all will work out for the best. I accepted the early buyout package to leave my employer before the factory shutdown. One, if I stay team members who do not have the energy to work as physically hard will want to use me to do their work. Two, it may be a wise move to get the jump on 2,500 people entering the job market, in the near future.

Session 06-08-2008. I moped around a little last week but I am now back on the upswing due to hormonal fluctuation hell. I was taught in a Women's Studies class that we all have them. I have not been taking magnesium and I ran out of vitamin D. The incorporation of magnesium and vitamin D usually helps me have fewer mood swings. Nutrition is essential! Please note, "These statements have not been evaluated by the Food and Drug Administration (FDA). These ideas are not intended to diagnose, treat, cure or prevent any disease," as they warn.

I took a drive to Charlotte today. It sure was nice to pass by the factory and smile broadly because I wasn't there. I feel like a freed slave. During this drive, I was rehearsing a conversation that I would like to have with Vaughn. In this conversation, I was explaining the x situation and y situation equals z due to these extenuating circumstances. These extenuating circumstance are because I am alone. I have always been alone. I have NEVER had anyone on which I could depend—not even in childhood to my recollection. As I ended the sentence of the prepared conversation, I was thinking my usual, "I have NEVER met anyone like me that has always been completely alone," when a song came on 91.9 with the first words being, "You're not alone, I've been waiting on you too long. . . here's where your heart belongs."—Main Stay, '*Where Your Heart Belongs.*'

MOOD CHANGE IN THE ZEITGEIST OF 2008

Session 06-19-2008 6:55 a.m. CNBC Squawk Box mentioned an upcoming episode about the top 1% having more wealth than 90% of the U.S. population combined. In one sense, you've got to admire it at its basic level. We are supposedly intelligent animals in the pursuit of passing on our genes, none-the-less—animals. It is evolution happening right before your eyes. With a sick and dying planet that is becoming incapable of sustaining all 6 to 7 billion of us, it is obvious that the top 1% will be passing on their genes and finding a way to provide for their descendants. It is all evolution—the evolution of energy. If we were truly human as distinguished from an animal, and not merely 'intelligent' animals along an evolutionary roller coaster, it would seem that we would help one another for the ability to bond with nature and The Creation/The Creator. You decide based on the evidence, in which classification we belong.

It's too many predators and too many who want to be at the top of the hierarchy. Some will stop at nothing in the pecking order. I believe the world would be better if we had more mutually beneficial (symbiotic) relationships. Are we the only species that prey upon each other, as if we are different? Those on the bottom are consumed for their energy to make profits for the top. It's cannibalistic.

An Italian proverb says, "After the game the king and the pawn go back into the same box." Agreeably, commenting on a photo of Earth from further out in our Solar System, Carl Sagan speaks best about this human condition quoted below:

> "The earth is a very small stage in a vast cosmic arena. Think of the rivers of blood spilled by all those generals and emperors so that in glory and in triumph they could become the momentary masters of a fraction of a dot. Think of the endless cruelties visited by the inhabitants of one corner of the dot on scarcely distinguishable inhabitants of some other corner of the dot. How frequent their misunderstandings, how eager they are to kill one another, how fervent their hatreds. Our posturing's, our imagined self-importance, the delusion that we have some privileged position in the universe, are challenged by this point of pale light. Our planet is a lonely speck in the great enveloping cosmic dark. In our obscurity—in all this vastness—there is no hint that help will come from elsewhere to save us from ourselves. It is up to us. It's been said that astronomy is a humbling, and I might add, a character-building experience. To my mind, there is perhaps no better demonstration of

the folly of human conceits than this distant image of our tiny world. To me, it underscores our responsibility to deal more kindly and compassionately with one another and to preserve and cherish that pale blue dot, the only home we've ever known."— Carl Sagan

DISAGREEING

Session 10-23-2008 7:27 a.m. The Yogi Bhajan conveys that, "If you are willing to look at another person's behavior toward you as a relationship with themselves rather than a statement about your value as a person, then you will (over a period of time) cease to react at all." After arguing with Keyché, I realize that my belief system is strong enough that I do not get irate when confronted with an opposing view. I did not mean to get into the topic of religious philosophy with her. It was unintentional. I then realized she is one of 'those people' that caused me to begin the documentation of my spiritual journey. Her brainwashed ignorance spews over the phone line as she tells me, "How stupid I am for having a higher education." Albert Einstein knew, "great spirits have often encountered violent opposition from mediocre minds." She continued to pop off, "I heard about people like you that get confused by higher education." I haven't the heart to tell her pea-sized brain that she is narrow-minded and needs to read more than one book. I was wrong in my internal assessment of her, as she was wrong in her vocal critique of me. Next time, I will try not to take things personally. "What people say about you is a reflection of them, not you,"—Author Unknown. "It requires less character to discover the faults of others than to tolerate them," instructs J. Petit Senn. In addition, Ralph Waldo Emerson advises, "For every one minute of anger, you lose 60 seconds of peace of mind." "Why argue? Often an argument only proves that two people disagree," from Moments Heartland Samplers. It also quotes "How painful are honest words! But what do arguments prove?"—The Bible, Job 6:25.

Session 10-25-2008 11:21 a.m. I don't fault you for your belief system as long as it makes you happy. If it doesn't make you happy—you're doing something wrong! Transforming Vision educates, "People who doubt their world view are restless and feel they have no ground to stand on. They are often in the throes of a psychological crisis. But the emotional crisis is fundamentally religious because our world view rests on a faith commitment." "Education is the ability to listen to almost anything without losing your temper," teaches Robert Frost.

Session 11-03-2008 5:01 p.m. There's got to be evolution. Otherwise, "we" would be at the top and the ultimate of creation. We would be the epitome and acting like it. Think about it, we can't be the top. It's not possible! We still act like savages. "The human species is not always a rational one, but we have managed to move along in a ragged march that for all its setbacks has been a steady climb from savagery to civilization, from subsistence to grand achievements," enlightens Jeffrey Kluger. I argue there is still a ways to go. My God—this can't be the top!

Think about the many ways we exhibit animal behavior. Many species mate for life. Some mate around. I've seen various animals steal food (resources) from their own. We flag and guard our territory and they mark and guard theirs. We've even seen them snuggling up under one another. Other than tools and communication, where is the difference? I would bet the Neanderthals thought they were the top, I'd bet the Greek and Romans thought they had created the highest civilizations and I'd bet the dinosaurs had a sense they were the top, too.

Session 11-06-2008. If we were that far above animals, wouldn't we help each other obtain higher levels of being to get closer to the Creator? We *are* animals! God gave us the ability to get to higher levels. Shouldn't we bring others along? "We all have one breath; man has no advantage over animals, for all is vanity, all go to one place" and Ecclesiastes 3:18-22 also asks, "Who knows if the spirit of men goes here and the spirit of animals goes there?"

ARE YOU POSITIVE OR NEGATIVE?

> Scientists sometimes study Rhesus monkeys to learn more about the human anatomy because there are certain similarities between the two species. While studying Rhesus monkeys, a certain blood protein was discovered. This protein is also present in the blood of some people (Rh+). Other people, however, do not have the protein (Rh-). The presence of the protein, or lack of it, is referred to as the Rh (for Rhesus) factor.—Unknown.

Most people are positive for the Rhesus monkey protein on their blood cells based on elementary mathematics. The other 15% of people must have lost this protein on the evolutionary ride. So, do you still believe you are too good to be distantly related to a monkey? Putting the idea of having a common ancestor with a monkey aside, we should all be able to agree that man has evolved from early man. Do you believe early man spoke or grunted and groaned? If you believe he spoke (I'll give you that) we can all see how language has evolved. Even if you look at only the English language, we speak differently than Shakespeare.

Our ways of communicating have evolved even faster. It has evolved from writing and having transcribers; to the printing press; to the typewriter; to the personal computer. Our use of the PC is based on the system of bits and bytes. Six bits equal a byte. A bit is a (1) or a (0) or an on and off signal. A certain series of bits make a letter A and a different series of bits make a letter B. We have evolved in our communications so vastly that we can use bits and bytes to send pictures and music. We can send this type of media wireless. This is what *we* can do. Therefore, is it not feasible to believe God Almighty can send a thought to our brains when He chooses, if you listen? Of course, if you believe early man grunted and groaned initially, nothing further needs to be said. You see the evolution.

Our Intelligent Designer designed the DNA sequence and put forth the utilization of it in His plan. For us to have evolved from early man, if not something similar to the other primates, our DNA sequences would have had to have small changes over time. Scientists call them random changes;

but it is possible that the Designer Himself can manipulate the changes as He sees fit—and it's easy for Him. He created the path and we can't go back.

Session 11-08-2008

I can't go back

To Africa I cannot go home

for there I am a mutt

A mixed breed

In need of roots

I do not know my Caucasoid ancestry

Slavery ended with that mystery

I have a dab of Mongoloid

A bit from the Native Americans

It is only reflected in my coarse hair

and two fingerprints that whorl

America is My World

for I was created here

I can't go back

God and infinite time

created in Africa the original condition of man

We sprang forth

Dispersed

And populated the Earth

into multifaceted

features and faces

colors and races

Most likely, Australia's Aborigines

resemble early man

Characteristics of the Big Three

Caucasoid

Mongoloid

and Negroid can be seen

In their island isolation—they were not

God was with them

The rest of us diversified

Multiplied

Then criticized the differences

Yet in me

The Big Three

have been reunited

Not equally

Yet,

still so beautifully

I will never know my roots

but I can still find my wings

to soar effortlessly

I can't go back

I was created here …

for God's purpose.

THE INAUGURATION OF HOPEFULNESS

Session 01-20-2009 9:14 a.m. As I sat watching the birds eating, I noticed they behaved more civilized than Man. A Jay, a Dove and a Cardinal were eating seeds by the side of the road. Oh, it's not a riddle—but it sure was nice to watch and it gave me tears of joy. Interesting how those three different species seem to coexist so effortlessly. I reckon it's a good thing the other Genus of Homo met with demise. After all, we are the same species separated by a variance of the skin pigment melanin and we use it as a divisive device. That is why I question; we're the top? We're still fighting for resources like 'lower' less intelligent forms of life; we're still competing for 'the prize' like sperm competition; we still watch as the weakest of us fall by the wayside—whilst, yes, whilst—the rest of the herd keeps pushing forward. Even Bertrand Russell agrees stating, "Collective fear stimulates herd instinct, and tends to produce ferocity toward those who are not regarded as members of the herd." How are we higher? How are we any different? Other than using sophisticated tools and communication, we are worse. We need to coexist as the Jays, Doves and Cardinals.
Session 03-07-2009 3:32 p.m. I was thinking about that quote from Havah, today. I'm supposed to "get something from this from God." The year is almost up. I am almost out of severance checks and I realized I might have made a mistake. I could have still been employed locally or in Richmond. Had I known we were in a recession when I made the decision, I may have made a different choice; but news of recessions comes out after the fact. This is no ordinary recession. It's the Great Recession. Author Michael Bernard Beckwith has been quoted saying, "When we're challenged, we can train ourselves to ask: 'what gift does this challenge bear?'" Todd B. Kashdan and Robert Biswas-Diener, *Psychology Today* also taught an insight on my decision. They said, "Purpose is what drives us to take risks and make changes—even in the face of hardship and when sacrificing short-term happiness." I learned least importantly, I'm a risk-taker. Sometimes it works out. Sometimes it doesn't. More importantly, I have turned from living life simply trying to survive to learning how to live for longevity. That alone has made this trying period the "something that I get from this from God," as Havah said.
Session 06-05-2009 8:00 a.m. Another beautiful morning and I have the windows open listening to the birds sing. I finally fed the birds. Times have been hard and money has been tight; so, I cannot purchase birdseed too frequently. Today I was glancing out of the window to see if any birds were eating this morning. At first, I did not see any. I thought as I listened,

"they're doing they're work." That seems to be their job. Watching the trees sway in the early morning breeze and listening to the music of the songbirds is awesome. During this Great Recession, it is my only source of contentment.

Session 10-08-2009 11:10 a.m. Today we bombed the moon. The President won the Nobel Peace Prize and I filled out a form W-4. Finally, an employer overlooked my youthful indiscretion. A great day and I slept with the television off, eliminated the distraction and enjoyed the peace. I've missed it.

Session 12-31-2009 9:30 a.m. I ran into that former co-worker, Havah, at my new place of employment. Thankfully, I could tell her that my 'ding' is called an eye flash (I also have a floater). I learned from Dr. Thomas before losing health insurance that had been provided with the severance package. I know she thought I was daft; but I'm glad I could tell her it was ignorance of the ophthalmologic medical condition. The eye flashes occurring with a spiritual thought caused me to infer The Spiritual. Lack of knowledge can lead to some well-placed false notions, even if it was in the most fitting moments.

MINUTES AND MOMENTS ARE NOTHING BUT TIME

Session 12-04-2006 10:40 p.m. "Every moment and every event of every man's life on earth plants something in his soul," according to Thomas Merton. Life is not short if you think of it in moments. I was thinking upon a time when I sat reading encyclopedias in the basement of my childhood home on Irving Street. That was a long time ago. In years, it was just a little over 30; but think how many moments have crept by? Corita Kent suggests, "Life is a succession of moments. To live each one is to succeed."

Session 07-05-2007. I had nothing but time on my hands while watching a Discovery Channel show titled, '*Before the Dinosaurs*,' the program, attempted to explain the Theory of Evolution as they see it before the time of the dinosaurs. The show discussed many interesting theories. As I watched, I realized it is more impossible to believe I am alive because of evolution. As scientific as they are and even if it does make sense to me, it is impossible to believe I exist because non-living matter did something chemically and began copying. Next, becoming a single celled organism then reproduced before dying. Then eventually a pre-fish reproduced before dying. I exist, today, because some fish type animal eventually became the first amphibians and began living on land. It is more impossible to believe that I exist because these animals gave rise to pre-mammals that produced the ape-like beings to which you, our simian cousins and I owe our lives. Simply because they had the *chance* to reproduce before dying, etcetera, etcetera, etcetera, over and over while natural selection and/or mutations changed little by little all descendants reproducing before death, throughout most of Earth's history. THIS is why I exist? It is less impossible to believe that God almighty reached down into the dust and created a man in our present form. It is less impossible to believe God made all as is; but think about it, who is the author of which story? Who wrote the simple story? Think about the infinite time that God has to create a more complex story. Whatever lies in our genetic makeup if it is true that we leapt from asexual reproduction to sexual reproduction it all seems to stem from the same plan. The same encoded information in our DNA passed down from our ancestors.

7
QUESTIONS REGARDING MY ANCESTORS

Through DNA testing, I have found a first to second cousin who is related to my father. The newly found cousin sent via text his dad's telephone number for follow up or potential leads. The (619) area code was an amusing coincidence. I also learned my combination of ethnicities. It is common knowledge that 60-80% of the African Americans in the United States have White, Native American or both in their ancestry. According to the Ancestry platform, thus far I'm the only chocolate stain in a DNA circle of vanilla.

Ultimately it goes back to Adam and Eve, or Mitochondrial Eve or even further. "All scientists agree that evolution has occurred - that all life comes from a common ancestry, that there has been extinction, and that new taxa, new biological groups, have arisen. The question is, is natural selection enough to explain evolution? Is it the driver of evolution?"—Lynn Margulis. Jeff Hawkins said, "And, you know, the fact is, if you believe in evolution, we all have a common ancestor, and we all have a common ancestry with the plant in the lobby. This is what evolution tells us. And, it's true. It's kind of unbelievable." "Most of our ancestors were not perfect ladies and gentlemen. The majority of them weren't even mammals."—Robert Anton Wilson

It matters not how God created it, whether God has hands in the push of evolution or if the story in Genesis 1 is correct. Genesis One is more in line with evolution because it tells God created the land, water, vegetation and creatures before creating "male and female, He created them."—Verse 27. The story written in Genesis chapter 2 is perplexing because it implies the all-knowing God did not have foresight when He realized the man should not be alone. Afterwards, it says God made a woman from the rib and side instead of hand-pattying a woman from the dust, as He did the man. What did He get lazy? I get angry when people insult the intelligence of God on one hand and profess God is all knowing on the other. Regardless, "with our knowledge of modern-day genetics, we realize that it was possible for God to place the potential for all people throughout history into the genes of Adam and Eve when He created them."—Walter Lang. Regarding the rib bone story, I would appreciate an answer to the question as to why men are creating dos equis. I am all woman and my contribution is XX. Males have XY and XX but it seems that they are in some part 'female' with some missing DNA on that Y chromosome. If it is true that XY is missing a little DNA, then we are all XX and apparently, sexuality is a continuum from the most feminine female to the most masculine male. I know because my ring finger is longer than my index finger. I don't know if The RZA expected me to interpret it in the way he answered Ari Melber saying, "The Y chromosome is random" but it does make me think these ideologies align.

Session 09-16-2016 6:19 a.m. While viewing a Through the Wormhole, hosted by Morgan Freeman, episode titled *Are There More Than Two Sexes* the blurred lines between genders was discussed. Information has been gained regarding the SYR gene SOX gene family and others as they relate to human gender and sexual reproduction. Genetic information confirms the human sexuality continuum.

DNA POINTING TO GOD'S PLAN

"The best book that has ever been written is in us and nowadays we have the opportunity to read it," says V. Utt of Estonia and an unknown author once said, "life is a whim of several billion cells to be you, for a while." I audited a genetics class at RCCC and I explained to the teacher how some people I've worked with think evolution theory is untrue. The teachers' response was that "evolution has been proven through DNA." It seems they are going on outdated data. "Facts do not cease to exist because they are ignored."—Aldous Huxley. One of the principles of Plato's Socrates is "Follow the evidence, wherever it leads."

Do you know how much DNA you have in common with a fly? I'm talking a fly that lands on feces and lays its eggs in carrion. The scientist who taught it said, "It's humbling." Stip, Knox and I have argued and I would reply, "A fly Mr. Order Primate but, you're too good to be related to a monkey?" Former atheist Antony Flew was quoted saying, "Biologists' investigation of DNA has shown, by the almost unbelievable complexity of the arrangements which are needed to produce (life), that intelligence must have been involved." "(It's) a structure of astounding elegance, a ladder delicately twisting into a double helix, packing into one efficient strand all the information to create a living being. No molecule in history has been more controversial."—G. Santis of Cyprus

I don't claim to know how or why The Creator made it that way. Only The Creator knows. "Not being able to comprehend what or why evolution occurs is probably a limitation of our imagination not a reason to discredit a theory."—Author Unknown. Neither science nor the church can unravel the mysteries of the universe. The key difference is the sciences make statements such as "we think" or "probably" from observation. The old ideology of the church tells us that it is this way because we say so and one must have 'faith' that the things being presented are true. I am more scientifically focused because no one is going to have me believe something based on his or her 'word.'

> Science is not only compatible with spirituality; it is a profound source of spirituality. When we recognize our place in an immensity of light-years and in the passage of ages, when we grasp the intricacy, beauty, and subtlety of life, then that soaring feeling, that sense of elation and humility combined, is surely spiritual. . . The notion that science and spirituality are somehow mutually exclusive does a disservice to both. — Carl Sagan

All forms of knowledge gained that we accept as true is based on trust in the authority of the source, but Transformed Thinking reminds us, "this does not mean, however, that we approach it superficially and uncritically."[xii] An Old Russian proverb, brought back to life by Ronald Reagan warns, "Trust but verify." Though science seems, to be more logical, and in many opinions closer to the truth—science still has work. Nevertheless, what is evolution but changes that occur in an organism over a long period of time? What does God (The Infinite; The Alpha and Omega; The beginning and the End) have plenty of?—TIME!

MATERIALISM AND GREED

Clean version:
The shallowness of man seems to me our greatest sin
What's everybody thinkin'? What race we tryin' to win?
We should spend our time and resources helping fellow men
Instead of wasting dollars on the latest fashion trend
What's cool for spring? What's hot this fall?
Be wise and share some wealth with all.
No white after Labor Day and that's out of style
No one really cares, if there's a hungry child?
Most Americans are suffering from obesity
Yet won't give a cup of rice to feed the least of thee
Who are you impressing with your thousand dollar purse
When it really comes down to it, what's it really worth?
Now I'm not completely saying we don't deserve the very best
My problem with the ways of our world is the absurdity of excess
I only have a problem with materialism and greed
How can one be so shallow, when so many are in need?
If you think you shouldn't believe me read Matthew twenty-five
And find out what our Savior taught when Jesus was alive
If you still do not believe me, I wouldn't really bet a buck
But if you make it to the Pearly gate, I'll say this once--Good Luck!

The first letter to John verse 3:17 tells us, "But whoever has this world's goods, and sees his brother in need, and shuts up his heart from him, how does the love of God live in him."

MINIMALISM

"My greatest skill in life has been to want but little."—Henry David Thoreau. Minimize excess and give more. You will enjoy the following insight from an unknown source sent via email.

> Enough
> What you have is enough. What you can do is enough. Right now, you have enough time, energy, knowledge, skills and resources to point your life in any direction. Once you begin the journey, as you need more, you'll find ways to bring it about. It's silly to wish for more when you could instead be making full use of what you have. Put your energy into creating the life you choose to live. Allow your inner self to be exactly where you would most like to be. And the rest of you will soon be there too. An endless abundance is yours if you simply choose to accept it. Fully accept what already is, and suddenly you have it all. Instead of wishing for more, bring to life the very best of the dreams that are already yours. Know that you already are enough, and discover just how magnificent it is.—Author Unknown, from a Daily Motivator sent via email to me from FAJ.

8
TEACHING US TO CONSUME TO SURVIVE

Session 07-12-2016 11:26 p.m. "Shhh!" I dreamed and awakened to the thought "If a man doesn't work a man doesn't eat; yet, if a man doesn't learn a man doesn't eat well." To this day, no one has put together the link between the lipid-panel ratio data and food allergies as it relates to hypertension. I'm trying to take some people on the journey to health through eye-opening information.

Session 09-16-2007 6:14 p.m. "Let thy food be thy medicine."—Hippocrates "Eat to live," preached the Honorable Elijah Mohammed (peace be upon him). Since first reading, I have remembered this bit of advice. It took a while before making the transformation; but I am well down the road to good health and a longer life. A friend once mentioned, "He chose to stop using his mouth as a garbage can." I used to eat all kinds of 'garbage' because of being underweight and no one taught me otherwise. I believed I could eat *anything* habitually, fried pork skins, chicken skin sandwiches (that's for you, Oprah), pork bacon, the fat around a Rib Eye Steak, and margarine/vegetable *spread* as a child. I preferred butter (spelled BUTTER not margarine) as an adult. Those who are health-conscious get the picture. I was eating to die. I asked God for guidance in getting my blood pressure under control then learned my bad cholesterol levels were high. Physiologically, ignorance is painful.

July 2006, Dr. Robert warned if I don't get my cholesterol under control I'll have to go on medication. I admitted to the doctor I'm addicted to fried food. He insisted, "Try using olive oil." I googled the benefits of olive oil then utilized his advice. I began documenting the 'coincidentally received' guidance I needed to restore health when I discovered a link. I learned about antioxidants and the reasoning behind the chemical processes that take place to combat free radicals and oxidation. I learned on whf.com the ten healthiest foods and from those how nutrients are taken into cells for them to do their work. Finally, I learned to decrease LDL cholesterol by avoiding the consumption of LDL causers and increase the intake of flax, olive and other beneficial oils.

During that time, I viewed an episode of *The Universe* on The History channel. I picked up the true weightiness of the word density. On the show, they discussed the density of a neutron star saying that, "a teaspoon would weigh (some quantity) ton." Prior DVR, I missed whether it was one ton or more because all I heard were the words *teaspoon and ton.*

In May 2007, it was time for a follow-up, which required fasting blood work. Shortly before the 12-hour fasting window, I swallowed a few tablespoons of Extra Virgin Olive Oil. My blood sample was taken the next morning. The following week the doctor wrote phenomenal on the results and no longer recommended medication. When telling the story, some responded I manipulated the results. My reply, no. It means consume some everyday.

Many have asserted canola and olive oils increase HDL, and the Cholestech Corporation study validates, "low levels of HDL actually increase your risk of coronary heart disease." It was really quite simple. Fortunately, I did not have any type of cholesterol disease or dis-ease so the God given natural oils did not 'cure' anything (that's for the FDA), but the denser (High Density Lipoprotein) oils possibly pushing the Low Density Lipoprotein out is a likely scenario. See the progress graphed below:

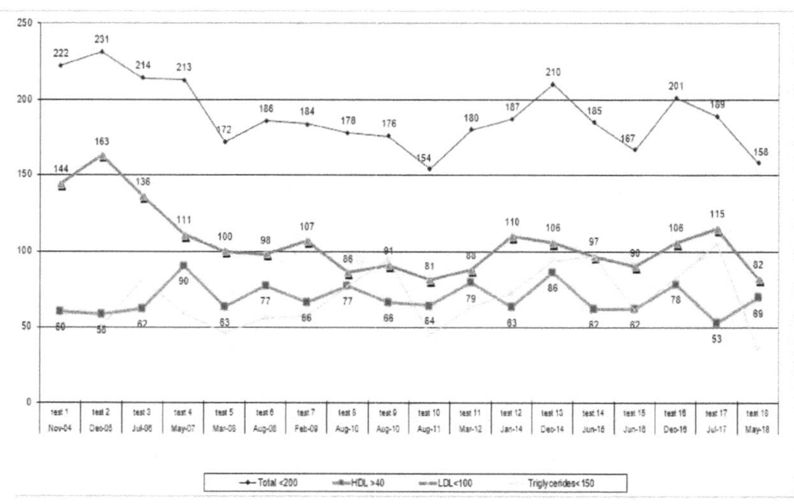

It may have something to do with the hypocrite, I mean Hippocratic Oath; but I find it interesting that many of our physicians will tell us the higher the HDL the better off we are, but they never expound on it. Ignorance is bliss, to those who profit from it. Mine did; but many physicians don't tell us to increase our High Density Lipoprotein we can simply consume healthy oils; but do recommend taking cholesterol lowering pharmaceutical drugs. *Is Your Heart at Risk* a brochure on knowing your HDL, verifies my speculation saying, "HDL cholesterol is considered your 'good' cholesterol because it can pick up 'bad' cholesterol and transport it to your liver, where your body can get rid of it." It further says, "High levels of HDL cholesterol can protect your arteries from cholesterol build-up (formed by 'bad' cholesterol) and reduce your risk of heart disease." Steven H. Horne, RH (AHG) and Dr. Kimberly Balas, ND, PhD. tell us, "The higher density lipoprotein is higher in protein." They further state:

> Cholesterol helps bind toxins, reducing inflammation and protecting nerve and brain tissue from chemical damage. Obviously, cholesterol is an important substance in the body, and necessary for our health. Excess cholesterol is not a cause of anything—it is a symptom that something is wrong . . . and the lipoproteins help engulf toxins. So the more toxins you have, the higher the cholesterol.

I value the truthfulness of that statement because as I (*not* utilizing that data) reduced my environmental toxicity, coincidently, my overall cholesterol declined—without exercise. They further state, "trying to lower cholesterol without trying to correct the real causes is just another example of modern medicine's tendency to treat symptoms without addressing the real causes." They also warn, "The lowest risk for cancer is when cholesterol is above 240 and cancer risk increases when cholesterol is below 140." That point I question. One could have 240 cholesterol and minimal consumption of antioxidant rich foods, which seemingly is a danger, as well.

It is one thing to read a brochure and think, "I've heard that before." It is quite another when you understand the reasoning behind the information and know how to utilize it in your everyday life. Increase consumption of flaxseed, walnut and olive oils and for a memory device the twenty-third Psalms tells us, "He anoints my head with oil." Yes, He anoints my head with oil and it is neither partially nor fully hydrogenated. If you're interested in the Biblical connection, BibleGateway.com has 202 search results. A few examples from the NIV version follow:

Exodus 30:32 calls oil sacred

Proverbs 21:20 in the house of the wise are stores of choice food and oil…

Isaiah 1:6 …soothed with oil

Mark 6:13 …anointed many sick people with oil and healed them

Deuteronomy 8:8 …a land with wheat and barley, vines and fig trees, pomegranates, olive oil and honey

Exodus 29:2 and Numbers 6:15 …from fine wheat flour, (no yeast), make bread and cakes mixed with oil, and wafers spread with oil

It was even used to pay a debt according to Luke chapter 16:5-7 …how much do you owe…eight hundred gallons of olive oil, but the debt was kindly reduced to four hundred gallons

Take notice of the many passages that explain the importance of oil. Don't let *them* continue to know something you do not. You know it now.

Session 09-17-2007 at 4:40 p.m. Is it confirmation or coincidence? The Oprah show was about eating healthy with Dr. Oz and TheBestLife.com pioneer Brian Greene. This confirms my belief that God is giving the guidance requested, through different media. Therefore, I sought more and learned of the creation process of partially hydrogenated oil, an LDL causer.

Treelight.com asks the question, "What is wrong with partially hydrogenated oils?" and answer boldly, "Consuming partially hydrogenated oils is like inhaling cigarette smoke. They will kill you—slowly, over time, but as surely as you breathe…and make you fat!" They also teach that fully hydrogenated oil becomes a solid (fat) because it acquires some hydrogen and becomes denser. However, I'm assuming not equivalent to the density one gets from the natural oils God made good.

Hydrogenated oils/oils that have had hydrogen added fully or partially (Trans fats) have had a growing realization that they are harmful. The MayoClinic.com verifies teaching, "Trans fats comes from adding hydrogen to vegetable oil." The first oil to have hydrogen added in mass production was the vegetable oil extracted from cottonseeds. Howtomakecandles.info confirms it was originally intended for candle production then utilized by a shortening manufacturer for food. I wonder if the executives at the company knew when naming it shortening—that they were making a product that would be shortening lives!

The deception comes when the inexpensive oils are only partially hydrogenated because stopping the full hydrogenation process of cottonseed oil is cheaper confirms, Treelight.com. I was getting ready to purchase one slice of chocolate cake until I read the frosting contained partially hydrogenated cottonseed oil. I was further educated that cottonseed oil usually contains pesticides because cotton is not considered a food source. Think about it and read food labels carefully!

It's ironic because hydrogen is not the villain. It's actually the lightest and most abundant element in the universe. We need it in the chemical compound that has two hydrogen atoms and one oxygen atom almost daily. Water is made that way by God and is in perfect balance with nature. Hydrogen infused in the oils that God made good is not a part of the natural equation. Oil that God created has been monkeyed around with. Man and his greed, created a less dense lipoprotein that is too light to be carried out of our arteries, therefore—getting stuck. Hence, the clogged arteries, heart attacks and strokes.

I once read an internet rumor about margarine being one molecule from plastic and flies will not hover around it. I had no scientific basis for believing it but I reasoned that if flies will not eat it and they eat shit, I would not knowingly put it in my mouth again. Before researching the data, that was one of my beliefs I held *almost* unreflectively. I now know hydrogenated oil was first intended for candles. The sheen on margarine and candle wax nearly resembles plastic. The word plastic means pliable and natural plastics are organic compounds harvested from the plant and animal kingdoms. I'm guessing there is some type of link between plastic and margarine, albeit stemming from natural organic compounds. Regardless, I have lost a taste for it. I conducted an experiment to corroborate the internet rumor. I left a container of partially hydrogenated oil outside in March of 2008. It was true. No flies swarmed around it and I had left it outside for a few weeks. The one fly that was found at the crime scene was dead. This is reminiscent of another internet rumor that hydrogenated oils were used to fatten up turkeys, but the turkeys were dying. A recent email prompted me to run the experiment again. I placed two containers of the 'stuff' outside about two weeks apart. The first container appears to have a dead mosquito in it and the other has no remains. The most remarkable thing about the experiment is that the 'stuff' yields no odor, no spoiling, nothing that a natural food source would do. So … if our bodies are machines to process and break down our intake of nutrients, then how can we metabolize something that the environment doesn't seem to be breaking down? It's not natural! On the third experiment, I placed three containers of spread and one container of real butter. The butter decayed within six weeks. The spread remained fifteen months later. I suggest you do so for yourself.

Session 11-09-2008. A good friend gave me an additional insight. Gene said, "Verify the flash point on the Trans fats, meaning does the temperature need to be over 100 degrees." If the hydrogen infused/trans-fat oils cannot be fully melted at a temperature below 100*ish* degrees, we should not eat it because our bodily temperature averages 98 degrees. If the fat is solid at room temperature, we should not consume it. I have flax oil that is liquid at 42 degrees. Stick with the oils in the liquid form that God intended, for good.

A scripture in The Bible says, ". . . your body is the Temple of The Holy Spirit placed there by God." Why would you put into that Spirit something nefariously man-made? Proverbs 12:18-19 corroborates, "the tongue of the wise promotes health and the truthful lip shall be established forever." Transform from merely saying, "What am I going to eat today?" to saying "What am I going to eat to *nourish* my body?" I mentioned above, in perfect timing God laid before me 'coincidently' all the materials I needed to improve my health to promote a longer healthier life. I hope this is 'coincidently' one of those pieces of information you may utilize to make healthy your life and nourish your soul. I have met people who believe God should have spared them from the consequences of poor diet choices. Some have a variety of ailments ranging from high overall cholesterol to cancers and bypass operations. One person said, "God gave me migraines." Some actually blame God for their health problems. God did not do this to us! We did this to each other and ourselves.

I thought no one would believe these insights. I may as well let them read the book. I realized a friend or acquaintance could have a heart attack, stroke or aneurysm before publication and I may be able to save a life. I began discussing ideas. I was pleased at how well the particulars were received. One man said he was proud of me. Most women said I never thought of it that way. My lifelong friend Danita remarked, "I prefer the taste of margarines and spreads because it is a lighter taste." I had to discuss with her the temperature data before she said, "I never thought of it that way!"

Session 11-10-2008. The talk show Morning Express on CNN reported the AMA is proposing a BAN on artificial trans fats. I only hope it will expose all of the code terms (margarine, spreads, hydrogenated oil, vegetable shortening) that mean *trans fats.*

Session 11-11-2008 6:33 a.m. In many countries, the norm is to drink hot tea or warm beer. I wonder about using so much *ice* in our country. Could it be a factor when consuming trans-fat laden foods that require a high degree melting point? What's more ridiculous is ice cream containing hydrogenated oil. What are they trying to preserve—ice cream is already frozen! It's ironic. Paying for hydrogen infused oil; while someone, who owns company stock is profiting; and in the meantime, killing poor people by marketing it as an alternative to butter with 'no cholesterol.' People are paying to be killed by clogging up their arteries and someone is making a profit!

Session 03-07-2009 8:34 a.m. I was putting together more of the puzzle so I'm not puzzled about the information I've digested. This week I collected the data from my last cholesterol check and my LDL was up a bit. It was due to rounding out the end of last year, being depressed and in a Deep Recession therefore I was less caring about my saturated fat intake. I did have a fish dinner or two from a local restaurant—so some 'plastic' may have slipped in. The great news is that my overall cholesterol has been reduced and my ratio (overall/to good) is still less than half the risk for heart disease (2.8) without exercise (though exercise is important because it "gets the stuff out of your blood and into your muscles," according to Dr. Robert). The ratio is a simple calculation of overall cholesterol divided by the HDL/good cholesterol. Knowing this information and utilizing elementary mathematics, it is a simple calculation to good health. Increase my HDL to 90+ via the oil of Olive, Walnut, Almond, Flax, etc. and divide overall by 90 for a ratio. See progress graphed below:

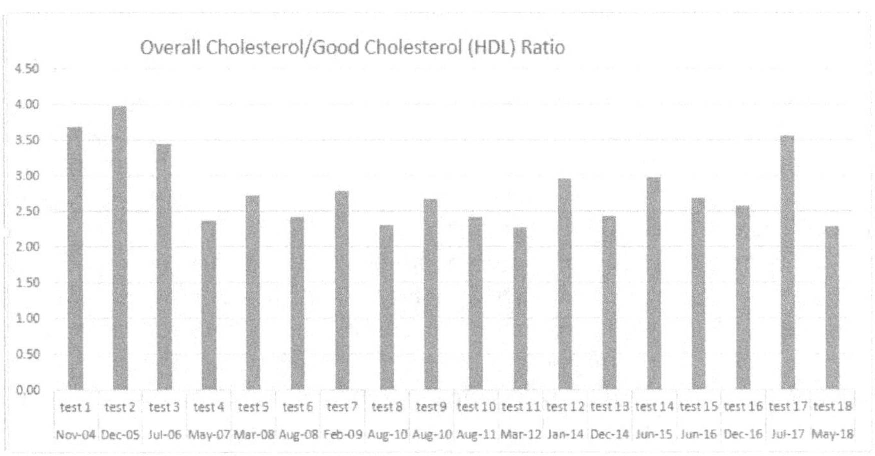

What are the benefits of a better ratio? For our 'protective' FDA, I say that the steps I have taken have not 'cured' any cholesterol disease (it's probably just a coincidence) for I know that correlation is not causation. I just wonder who *they* are protecting—The American people or The American people who own stock in the pharmaceutical companies and packaged food industry. It seems to me the US government is the biggest drug pusher of all.

It's great that I gained most of this information from reading. Reading is *fundamental;* that is Fun, da?!? and mental. The sad thing is the people who need this information most, most likely will not read it.

Session 12-19-2009 7:30 a.m. It takes quality parts to make a quality machine. There is a world of difference between a Mazda6 and a Mercedes. If we go from saying grow to make, it would make a whole world of difference in the way we treat our bodies. Think about it. We say we grow older, we grow food, we grow a garden, and we grow hair and nails. However, we make new hair and nails. Make. The carrot seed made new carrots and new carrot seeds from the instructions placed in the DNA. Again, I refer to "The body being temple of the holy spirit placed there by God." What could make the instructions that made the machinery/body/Temple that houses the Holy Spirit . . . but God? Knowledge is power. Power lies in knowing, not who but, what you are!

Session 01-01-2010. California has banned trans fats in restaurants, though it's still allowed in baked goods. As far as I know, New York City was next to institute a ban. The rest of the country will probably be slow to the bandwagon. The quicker we die the less chance of having our Social Security money returned after having it taken from us for fifty years. Most likely, China and India will begin pumping their citizens full of the stuff. After all, it's population control. It's supposed to be nine billion of us by 2047, but if they continue administering the 'shortening' it may help stave off the mass infestation of humanity. It's more subtle than Raid®.

Session 01-07-2010. The Daily Show with John Stewart had an author speak on how the hydrogenated oil and high fructose corn syrup industries are subsidized by the government. I was wrong to write The White House, contact my Congressman and Senators suggesting a tax on the foods that are detrimental to health as way to raise capital for the 'health care bill.' Our tax dollars already support the opposition.

Session 06-09-2010 9:16 p.m. The information enciphered in the DNA enables us to decipher external data for gaining more information. One example is the debate surrounding organics. When I put into my temple organic celery, the ribbing has superior strength. The strength of the organics versus wimpy non-organic—I want that strength to be used to make my new parts! Moreover, it fits because I'm made of that (the chemical components of the celery stalk). When you put into your temple (plastic), i.e. hydrogenated oils and other long chemical names and you don't know what they are—it doesn't fit, doesn't fit chemically, so you are thrown off balance. You're not made of that. The instructions programmed in the DNA allow us to translate external data for gaining more information. Now that we have these instructions (DNA) why shouldn't we use instructions (good data) that keep the machinery making quality parts and/or a quality house/temple of the Holy Spirit. What it all boils down to is . . . I've got my new instructions as to what I put into my mouth. I've got my orders, from the Holy Spirit that is in me, placed there by God. I can't control the economy, I can't control the government, industry or capitalism; but what I can control is my right hand to my mouth.

Session 07-08-2016 6:08 a.m. A little after midnight on July 5th, I was checking my blood pressure on a machine at a local grocery store. Initially it would not give a reading. I had to acknowledge the warning that instructed go to the emergency room immediately. The machine displayed 200/120. I retested. The warning also asked, "If I felt chest pains, labored breathing or lightheadedness?" Well, I knew something was off; but I wasn't worried about any of those issues. In fact, by looking at the chart way above, my most recent lipid panel was good and my overall cholesterol to HDL ratio was 2.7. That is well below the warning ratio that would cause concern, and my doctor recently told me I may be able to stop taking medication.

I drove to the ER and parked my car. As I walked in, I felt lightheaded. The receptionist asked, "What are you here for?" As I explained, she asked the same questions the machine had asked. I told her I felt lightheaded walking from the car but not until the machine told me to look for that indication, I said jokingly. I assumed that if the receptionist sits me with the rest of those waiting, it was not that much of an emergency. "Johnson," the nurse said. I was tested. The machine seemed to malfunction. The attendant said, "I've never seen the machine do that before." When the machine finally took my reading it was only 182/110, twenty and ten points below the machine at the store. My crisis was urgent but not an emergency. The triage nurse finally came in to ask questions about my day and asked me about food allergies. I gave her details from my day. I also told her I had just received annual exam results that it's unlikely I would have a stroke or heart attack. That night the emergency room was packed; so, there were no beds available. I told her that in a few hours, it will be time to take my medicine, so if I'm to wait here for too long, I may as well go home and take the regularly scheduled dosage. She let me sign a waiver and released me.

At home, I heard my friend Maerin's voice convey, "That's probably why your blood pressure was up" regarding a time last fall when I had angioedema. I googled food allergies and hypertension and the information was right there at my fingertips. I'm now convinced and I am going back on Dr. Peter D'Adamo's "Blood Type Diet," which I had previously followed religiously. I admire Dr. D'Adamo. In a civilization that believes the world is flat, he is showing us that it is round.

Peer pressure, at work, caused me to be far less stringent and I eventually gave up on his recommendations. That day I consumed coffee, milk, potatoes, pork, pickles, vinegar, and peppers (which according to D'Adamo I can eat; but was my most recent suspicion for angioedema). My predisposition for hypertension may be activated by allergens. I wonder what would have happened had my lipid panel been more in line with an average American in conjunction with my allergen reaction.

My co-workers think I'm strange again for not following herd mentality; but, whom should I trust my fellow button pushers or the man with the Ph.D.? They laugh; but as far as health is concerned, it doesn't seem their plans are working. I have to ask myself, "Who's the stupid one, at least they don't know any better?" I discussed it with Trent and we laughed. He breaks in, "Who are you going to believe?" I said, "Smart people!" Conversely, we should thank my peers because if not for them, I would not have had the epiphany and you would not have this new knowledge. I described what happened; yet, they still laugh. When I learn, I want to teach. I guess my voice is loudest, when it's written down. What drives me to do this? My desire to teach those who won't listen. I repeat, "My voice is LOUDEST, when it's written down."

"Knowledge is of no value unless you put it into practice."—Anton Chektov. I know how to utilize what I've read regarding the metabolic processes and what role it plays on our genes. People have a misunderstanding about genetics. I refuse to accept the diagnosis of hypertension. I may have a genetic predisposition for High Blood Pressure; but I do not have to turn it on. Many do not know anything of epigenetics and the new information that is available. My predisposition is synonymous with the susceptibility Dr. Peter D'Adamo speaks of regarding an 'avoid' food that may cause flocculating serum or precipitating serum proteins. Dr. D'Adamo trains us as to when a food "Contains a component which can modify known disease susceptibility" which leads to the allergic and inflammation responses. One can google "*An overview of adverse food reactions*" and The World's Healthiest Food website will corroborate these claims.

Rudy Rivera, M.D. and Roger D. Deutsch discuss the ALCAT test, of which physicians are aware, in their book titled, "*Your Hidden Food Allergies are Making You Fat.*" They briefly mention Dr. D'Adamo on page 97 where they concur his ideology "may give general information …but; is too nonspecific …" I argue, at least it is a guide. However, they do agree, "Further research of the relationship of blood types to food sensitivities and other predispositions may yield valuable information." Most importantly, they assert, "Food allergies are more strongly associated with heart attacks and strokes than cholesterol results." That is powerful reinforcement of something I discovered for myself. Albert Einstein reminds me, "Any fool can know the point is to understand," while F. Scott Fitzgerald informs, "Genius (I prefer brilliance) is the ability to put into effect what is on your mind." I am thankful that what is on my mind comes from the great minds of others.

As far as the FDA, this is just *my* story; so, don't think your secret is out. I do know one thing. It is testable and measurable. I guess everyone's health will eventually improve because the Food and Drug Administration announced on June 16, 2015 that they will no longer allow 'them' to administer hydrogenated oil to us and it will be outlawed by 2018 saying, "that partially hydrogenated oil is no longer generally recognized as safe." The manufactures need a three-year window to reformulate products and minimize profit loss. Though only after putting their noses into our health care, have 'they' become concerned about strokes and heart attacks. Why, suddenly, have they stopped agreeing with the food industry in favor of the insurance industry? Can they no longer kick us off health care plans? The things humans do for profit or the protection of.

For the protection of is correct. Two thousand eighteen came and went. As new political administrations come, there that goes. Enjoy your hydrogenation!

I hope this information will save the life of someone who will save some lives! If we nourish our bodies and minds, the mind begins to function properly and we can change bad habits of consumerism, materialism and greed to having a desire to succeed.

9
CHOOSE TO SUCCEED

Shall I succeed, Albert Pike reminds, "What we have done for ourselves alone dies with us; what we have done for others and the world remains and is immortal." Michael Hyatt's website confirms; "You are not born a winner. You are not born a loser. You are born a chooser." James Lane Allen said, "Adversity does not build character. It reveals it!" "It is your reaction to adversity, not the adversity itself that determines how life's story will develop"—Dieter F. Uchtdorf. "Nothing goes to waste on the journey of life. Both good and bad experiences shape your mind and heart for what is to come."—Leon Brown. "All successful people, men and women, are big dreamers. They imagine what their future could be, ideal in every respect, and then they work every day toward their distant vision, that goal or purpose."—Brian Tracy.

"He conquers, who endures," by Perseus was updated when Usher told Oprah and the audience, "You succeed as a result of sticking to it." Harper Lee advises, "Many receive advice, only the wise profit from it." Accordingly, Hagakura cautions, "one must edge forward like the inchworm, bit by bit," for "the race is not always to the swift but to those who keep on running."—Ecclesiastes. "Slow and steady wins the race"—Aesop, because "in the long run, a short-cut seldom is."—Malcolm Forbes.

Unguided would describe my youth, though I survived grades first through sixth fairly well having received good grades. Junior high and high school, I did not. After three years of skipping school and passing, I had a reintroduction to the tenth grade that prompted my mom's half-sister to send me to North Carolina. My first day in town I found a job with the intention of returning to D.C. Working part-time and my established habit of skipping school landed me another invite to the tenth grade. I declined the invitation. Luckily, I tested on twelfth grade level and received my adult High School diploma in three months—the same year I was supposed to graduate had I not been invited to the tenth grade thrice. I almost fell into the trap; but I chose to overcome learned helplessness, which Dr. Phil cautions, "It's when you get to believe that there's not a lot you can do to change your plight in life." Fortunately, once I went to college, school became almost as easy as it was during elementary. I know that had I been groomed properly, the possibilities would have been different—maybe better.

Stephen Covey enlightens, "Live out of your imagination, not your history." Statistically, I was not supposed to make it. In my lineage, I have four times great grandparents who were slaves. I was born on the 102nd anniversary of Juneteenth (6/19): the day my ancestors celebrated their "freedom" for the first time following 246 years of enslavement dating back to 1619. My four times great grandmother Nancy Roseman was born enslaved. She named my three times great grandfather Sam. I have three times great grandmothers, Mary Jane (Sam's wife) and Esther who were born just outside of American slavery. Via the Ancestry platform, I discovered I have Ayers DNA, yet the Willeford/Williford family name. One distant Caucasian cousin has her family genealogy showing Arden Jered Williford married Mary Ann "Queen" Ayers. Queen's father was Samuel Ayers and his father was Captain John "Jack" David Ayers. I'll never know if my ancestors were on the Ayers plantation then sold to the Willifords or if the Ayers 'gentleman' visited the slave quarters on the Williford plantation. I do know one thing. DNA was left at the crime scene. DNA can prove you've committed a crime. However, it can't prove you're related to the slave masters descendants as they say, "*If* it's true . . ." During that time more likely some of the slave mothers were preadolescent then shortly after post-pubescent girls because the ages and dates are 'all out of whack' in the timeline.

My great great grandmother, Sallie Willeford White, was raised in The South through The Great Depression. She was in a house fire and died in a segregated hospital. Since my great grandmother was raised on the crux of these issues, she was miserly—as if it were my fault, I had to eat. I'd always think, "I ain't ask to be here." I wasn't too fond of her. I was eighteen when she passed. I never shed a tear. Her daughter was my alcoholic grandmother whom I liked, (she showed me an infinitesimal amount of love, especially when she had a swig) but she was married to an abuser. His beatings coupled with her alcoholism killed her before age 52. My mom was mentally challenged and I have no idea of the 'gentleman' that took advantage of her child-likeness that produced my conception; but I guess I should thank him. I don't know why she had not been prevented from bearing children. Perhaps, some laws against it. No one thinks of the children and the suffering we must endure. I don't know if she had always been child-like due to (possible) fetal alcohol syndrome or the stroke she had in her twenties. Barbara Ann returned to the Oneness of The Universe when she was only 42. My mom had a half-sister that did not care about anyone but herself. I don't know her story but maybe there was a reason she resorted to self-preservation—some in our bloodline lack the empathy gene. When Barbara Ann died, I didn't bother telling her or my cousin, because no one cared.

I may be a bit of a sociopath, because I never felt ashamed for employing thievery to eat. When I turned 16, I worked two jobs, SYEP and a well-known fast food chain restaurant earning the $3.35 minimum wage.

Consumed with anger and the fear of homelessness motivated me to eke out a living.

Eventually, Suze Orman taught me "anger, fear and shame are barriers to wealth." Growing up under the aforementioned circumstances, I was supposed to fail. Fortunately, God kept his Word and placed in me the appetite that Les Brown instills, "If you take responsibility for yourself, you will develop a hunger to accomplish your dreams." "When my father and mother forsake me He will adopt me," says Psalms 27. Apparently, He did because the chips were stacked against me. I have had no support system—only being the one from whom everyone wanted support. I guess they saw my strength. My kindness they mistook for weakness—yet; all the while God was with me. When some attempted to make a mockery of me, God in His infinite wisdom was kind enough to use it for good. God helped me choose to succeed. The grace of God strengthened me even when I did not know. Nelson Mandela enlightens:

> Our deepest fear is not that we are inadequate. Our deepest fear is that we are powerful beyond measure. We ask ourselves, who am I to be brilliant, gorgeous, talented and fabulous? Actually, who are you not to be? Your playing small doesn't serve the world. We were born to make manifest the glory of God that is within us. And as we let our light shine, we unconsciously give other people permission to do the same.—Nelson Mandela

Ben Sweetland's quote complements, "We cannot hold a torch to light another's path without brightening our own."

The quotes in this book have taught me. "Teachers open the door. You have to enter by yourself."—Chinese Proverb. I was supposed to fail—but I didn't, at least not too badly. That's God. "God will not look you over for medals, degrees or diplomas, but for scars."—Elbert Hubbard "Though He gives you the bread of adversity and the water of affliction, yet He will be with you to teach you—and with your eyes you will see your Teacher." Isaiah 30:20[xiii] "We rejoice in the hope of the glory of God. We also rejoice in our sufferings, because we know that suffering produces perseverance; perseverance, character; and character, hope"—Romans 5:2-4 NIV. Rita Mae Brown once said, "Never hope more than you work;" but hope is exactly what we need for the future.

CREATE THE FUTURE

I am going to reign over my own destiny because my name means noble. "The best way to predict the future is to create it"—Peter Drucker. In developing an intimate and personal relationship with God, utilizing ideology from '*The Secret*' then coupling them with biblical scripture as well as other ideology, I put together a puzzle and no one knew it was right but me. I may be overconfident; but "delusions of grandeur make me feel a lot better about myself."—Jane Wagner.

Astronomy, mathematics, physics, chemistry, geology, anthropology, and biology—it too, fits together like a puzzle. Each of these disciplines are linked together and they all point to an Intelligent Designer. If you cannot accept that—you cannot deny that it is a heck of a design. Evidently, I am correct in my assessment, because you have become an accomplice in my mission. The proof is the fact that you are reading this right now; though, it helps having a chorus of others to hide amongst when you cannot hit every note well.

"I have learned this, at least, by my experiment: that if one advances confidently in the direction of his dreams, and endeavors to live the life which he has imagined, he will meet with a success unexpected in common hours."—Henry David Thoreau. Wayne Dyer teaches, "Our intention creates our reality" while Anais Nin makes known, "we are beginning to see the influence of dream upon reality and reality upon dream." I want to become an author. I want to be as Steve Jobs declared, "Put a ding in The Universe." "The mode in which the inevitable comes to pass is through effort"—Oliver Wendell Holmes and "visualizing your results is the key to realizing your results."—James Ray

Session 05-05-2013. Utilizing the above principles, I must continue with the work. Work in equals results out. I should "never give up on something I can't go a day without thinking about" warns Winston Churchill, because "all who have accomplished great things have had a great aim, have fixed their gaze on a goal which was high, one which sometimes seemed impossible," according to Orison Sweet Marden. "It does not matter how slowly you go so long as you do not stop," Confucius said. Also, I remembered from viewing '*The Secret*' the sentence, "you create your own destiny as you go along." The video tells us that Winston Churchill said, "You create your own universe as you go along." Joyce Meyer similarly agrees, "Your destiny unfolds as you take steps." Take steps to make it happen! However, take sensible steps and do not to put the cart before the horse, as I.

President Barack Obama, to his audience, once advised, ". . . Our kids can't all aspire to be LeBron or Lil' Wayne." I have a few degrees; but I have only been good at working. I cannot figure out how to open a business, though I've been taught to write a business plan. I have learned you must find that thing, if but one, that you're good at and put in the time. It may be 10,000 hours or more; but they may be the down payment for success. Some examples of people who put in the time are Alicia Keys, Yanni, Prince, Panic at the Disco, 21 Pilots, Neil DeGrasse Tyson, Peyton Manning and Steph Curry to name a few. How many hours would you guess that they put into perfecting their crafts? Bach, Beethoven, Copernicus, Galileo, Carl Sagen and maybe even Michael Jordan did not have to contend with as many distractions as we have today. Therefore, to put the time in for results out is commendable.

My only thing was getting decent grades on research papers and finding commonality in the seemingly unrelated. Winston Churchill imbues, "Continuous effort, not strength or intelligence, is the key to unlocking your potential" and Earl Nightingale reminds, "Never give up on the dream just because of the time it will take to accomplish." By using my passion for words, I can create something great. Henri Frédéric Amiel declared, "Without passion a man is a mere latent force and possibility, like the flint which awaits the shock of the iron before it can give forth its spark."

> "You are a creator; you create with your every thought. You often create by default, for you are getting what you are giving your

> attention to wanted or unwanted. Your feelings will tell you if you are creating what you want or what you don't want. Where is your attention focused?"—Abraham Hicks.

Golo Mann enlightens, "Man is always more than he can know of himself; consequently, his accomplishments, time and again will come as a surprise to him." Henry Thomas Hamblin wrote, "The creative power can be so highly developed that a sick man can make himself well, a poor man can change his circumstances from poverty to prosperity, and a miserable and despondent pessimist can change himself into a cheery, optimist" because "life isn't about finding yourself. Life is about creating yourself."—George Bernard Shaw. Have I created the future? Did it work?

THE CULMINATION

While speaking with my Pastor 04-22-2007, I was trying to articulate how I've attempted to share my spiritual growth and how most times many do not understand what I'm attempting to convey. The Pastor said, "They're scared." I did not ask him to elaborate because I thought I knew exactly what he meant. I read the introduction of Neale Donald Walsch's book July 7, 2007 and he agrees by saying, "We are all led to the truth for which we are ready."[xiv] My friend Knox reminded me of a Bob Marley quote that goes, "emancipate yourself from mental slavery; none but ourselves can free our minds." The Illustrated World's Religions subtitled A guide to Our Wisdom Traditions has a quote from Buddha which falls in line with the above reasoning. It confirms:

> In his (Buddha's) later years, when India was afire with his message, people came to him asking what he was. Not "Who are you?" but "What are you?"
>
> "Are you a god?" they asked.
>
> "No."
>
> "An angel?"
>
> "No."
>
> "A saint?"
>
> "No."
>
> "Then what are you?"
>
> Buddha answered, "I am awake."

I felt that fear, which is a spirit of evil, trying to cause me to have doubts during my writing process. I shut that fear and doubt out. Finally, do not be alive to religion and spiritually dead. Lose that 'devil'! Lose the fear, which is a spirit (not apparition) of evil, and meet God.

Follow Matthew 25 and Proverbs 10:16 doing good with your blessings, document progress and see what happens. When you do ask God to use you, you can be assured that it does work and it is documented as, "The Lord is good and glad to teach the proper path to all who go astray; He will teach the ways that are right and best to those who humbly turn to Him."—Psalm 25:8-9 [TLB]

Without a doubt, this will be the impetus to propel us out of the spiritual dark ages. "Truth will ultimately prevail where there is pains to bring it to light"—George Washington. Our time will be known as the Spiritual Dark Ages. Let us awaken so we don't have to remain in spiritual darkness for another few hundred years!

10
BERT III
THE REEMERGENCE OF DOUBT

"He was a wise man who invented God."—Plato. Session 02-03-2010. Two plus years later, common sense tells me I was so interested in Creation and so high on God that I saw the miraculous in the mundane. Reminding me, if you put God on your mind you will find God there.

> The Greek philosopher (BC 341-270), Epicurus asked:
> "Is God willing to prevent evil, but not able?
> Then he is not omnipotent.
> Is he able, but not willing?
> Then he is malevolent.
> Is he both able and willing?
> Then whence cometh evil?
> Is he neither able nor willing?
> Then why call him God?"

Isaiah 45:7 of The Bible conversely answers, "I form the light and create darkness. I make peace and create evil. I the Lord do all these things."

Worst-case scenario is—this is it, as I stare into the darkness of a bedroom furnished mostly with plastic. Perfectly positioned between the good life and suffering, at times, I am still less than satisfied. I must remember my principles. I dislike materialism and greed. I understand that with all that I do have, it is only my perception of lack that is causing me to feel unsatisfied. I am aware of the importance of minimalism; therefore, I have much of which to be appreciative. "Not until we are lost do we begin to understand ourselves."—Henry David Thoreau. Natalie Gulbis said, "When you fail, you learn from the mistakes you made and it motivates you to work even harder."

THE ACTUAL DISCOVERY

Session 01-02-2009 2:20 p.m. This is all we get! Even if there were no heaven, nothing more than this, you're still a part of God. You are still a part of Creation. One cannot trust faith alone. It's too many predators.

Session 01-03-2009. I was thinking back on a few associates that, in my opinion, have used faith improperly. I remember a couple of them missing mortgage payments yet paying tithes. Another remarking on what *all* they have acquired because of their belief system and faith. I never used my faith in that manner; however, I did have faith that if I do well in helping others that God would see to it that all would turn out well for me, since my heart was, as '*they*' say, in the right place.

I have not had the ability to give in a way that would be life changing for the receiver. I admire the people who become philanthropist and behave as Proverbs 10:16 tells us, "The good man's earnings advance the cause of righteousness. The evil man squanders his on sin." "Selfishness is the path to misery, but selflessness is the key to experiencing life at its fullest"—Author Unknown. Matthew 25 teaches, "What you have done for the least of these of my brethren you have done for Me."

When I began earning a living wage, I was dolling out too much money to people for the wrong reason—consumerism. A quote attributed to Henry Ford is a lesson I learned too late. He taught, "Givers have to set limits because takers seldom do." Similarly, Michelle Roya Rad, MA, Psyd. advises, "One must have a rational mind that makes the person adept as to when to give, what to give and to whom to give; without damaging the self." Proverbs reads, "Diligence leads to profit as surely as haste leads to poverty." Unfortunately, I let my ignorance and the predators get the upper hand. So …

Session 01-04-2009 6:50 p.m. If you don't manage faith properly, it can lead to foolishness. I had to be kicked, beaten, consumed by the predators, crawled back bloodied and bruised simply to have a new mattress and a bath that *remained* hot make me feel like a queen—only to discover: Financially, ignorance is painful. Dr. Geoff paraphrased a Ben Franklin quote, "We are all born ignorant; it takes a lot of hard work to stay that way."

Session 01-24-2009. Faith used improperly will flub you up. I use to be a 'what if' type of thinker. Listening to the religious pundits, I began believing the hype. After massive failures utilizing that thought process, I have returned to realizing that I must be a 'what-if' type of thinker. I must use cost/benefit analysis and risk-reward methodologies. This coming full-circle does not affect my understanding of my place in The Creation. Through this growth cycle, I have become a happier person. I had business sense—but no faith. I gained faith and lost common business sense. I gave up being pragmatic for hope and faith. What if I heard Huey Freeman say, "Hope is irrational" beforehand? I also needed to know Galileo's quote "I do not feel obliged to believe that the same God who has endowed us with senses, reason and intellect has intended us to forgo their use." I wish I had learned sooner that, "Ignorance is not bliss. Ignorance is poverty. Ignorance is devastation and ignorance is illness. It all stems from Ignorance," says Jim Rohn. It was tough to endure. "Experience is a hard teacher because she gives the test first, then the lesson afterward."—Vernon Sanders Law. On the flip side, "Good judgment comes from experience. Experience comes from bad judgment."—Tom Watson. I remember once working twenty feet high on a scissor lift praying and hoping for something, when I heard that inner voice tell me "I'm here for matters of the spirit." I didn't want to hear it! It was counterintuitive to my belief system at the time; so, I had to learn from bad judgment.

"In order to love who you are, you cannot hate the experiences that shaped you."—Andréa Dkystra. I love me and my best days are ahead! As far as the little asymmetrically faced girl whom no one loved that always seemed to be alone, I love it and agree with Henry David Thoreau's quote, "I find it wholesome to be alone the greater part of the time. To be in company, even with the best, is soon wearisome and dissipating. I love to be alone. I never found a companion that was so companionable as solitude." However, the world can be lonely without another set of eyes.

"If you're looking for a happy ending and can't seem to find one, maybe it's time you start looking for a new beginning instead . . ."—Ritu Ghatourey. I can successfully execute an idea, profit from it while working and end up at the same place (financially speaking) I was supposed to have been had I followed a traditional course. I know I can, because I've done it before. Within me, the two, faith and common business sense have been united. I now keep matters of my Spiritual World and matters of my physical world separate. I am whole and at peace with Emmanuel who continually tells us, "I am not who you think I am; you are who you think I am."—Unknown.

Whether by grace of God, coincidence or serendipity, I ran into Havah while taking an assessment test for a new job. She and I were in the first group of twenty applicants to complete all requirements and the possibility of us being together again, in the same building, seemed as if we had "got that something we were supposed to get from God." I was hired at the company that purchased the building from the employer that had the mass layoff. Havah and I working together in green technology would have been a nice ending; but she continued on her own path when I was hired at Atevlu, April 4, 2016. The place was wrecked so I went back to my other job after vacation. Due to my fragmented, dysfunction, unstable life, I long for stability and Atevlu was in its infancy. I had two full time jobs and two empty lockers. April 29, 2016, I visited 1300 in Brookland and everything looked smaller, yet clean. The streets were wrecked; funny, they only needed fresh blacktop.

May 22, 2019, I was hired at a company seemingly equivalent to the factory that closed, as far as work hours, how the employer treats employees and cleanliness is concerned.

Session 06-19-2019. Almost twelve years to the day, I said to the CEO and audience at the tobacco factory, "When God closes one door He opens another. I've enjoyed the ride," I looked up at the computer monitor at the receiving desk and saw a taped Chinese cookie fortune that reads, "When one door closes, another will open."

ABOUT THE AUTHOR

Alberta Johnson is the Chairman of the Board, President and CEO of 619 Sessions, Inc., a publication and baked goods manufacturing company. She earned two Associates degrees from Rowan-Cabarrus Community College and a Bachelor's of Business from Montreat College.

---

[i] Walsch, Neal Donald Conversations with God an uncommon dialogue G.P. Putnam's Sons New York, NY 1995

[ii] Curtis. E.M., Brugaletta, J., (200). Transformed Thinking. Franklin, Tennessee: JKO Publishing. Page 29

[iii] Grenz, Stanley J., (1998). Created for Community. Grand Papids, Michigan: Baker Books page 18, 11, 14

[iv] Glassford, Darwin K., (1998). A Concise Introduction to a Biblical Worldview. Montreat, NC: Montreat College. Page 3

[v] Proverbs 20:24

[vi] Biology concepts and connections. Campbell, Mitchell and Reece The Benjamin/Cummings Publishing Co. 1997 page 34

[vii] New King James Bible, James 1:21

[viii] NIV Bible, James 1:21

[ix] Amplified Bible, James 1:21

[x] The Holy Bible, John 1

[xi] The Holy Bible, John 17:21-23

[xii] Curtis. E.M., Brugaletta, J., (200). Transformed Thinking. Franklin, Tennessee: JKO Publishing. Page 20

[xiii] The TLB Bible Isaiah 30:20

[xiv] Walsch, Neale Donald, "Conversations with God" Introduction page. G.P. Putnam's Sons New York, NY 1995

www.ingramcontent.com/pod-product-compliance
Lightning Source LLC
Chambersburg PA
CBHW070500130626
46555CB00003B/1094

9780578530697